THE SILVER TYPHOON

By Robert Sidney Bowen

I0549219

ALTUS PRESS • 2017

DUSTY AYRES AND HIS BATTLE BIRDS:
THE SILVER TYPHOON

CHAPTER 1
S.O.S.

TWISTING AROUND in the seat, Dusty stared back at the two sleek X-Diesel monoplanes sticking to his elevators as though they were glued there. In the orange-peel cowled cockpit of one was the lean, wiry figure of Curly Brooks. In the other, the hefty, stevedore hulk of Biff Bolton. Across the air space he saw both of them grin and salute smartly—thumb to nose, fingers extended vertical.

He returned both the grin and salute with gestures, turned front again and shot his ship straight down toward the home drome of High Speed Group 7, directly below. A couple of thousand feet off the drome, he eased back on the stick and curved the ship up and over in a gigantic loop.

At the peak he rolled off, doubled back and thundered into a perfect outside loop. Again he rolled out, this time on the bottom side, streaked forward with bullet-like swiftness, and turned in the seat.

Curly and Biff were still grinning, and still clinging to his elevators. Dusty nodded, reached out a hand, and flipped on radio contact.

"Not bad, children," he grunted into the transmitter tube. "Not bad at all. O.K., the field. Last one down, stands the drinks!"

Half a minute later Dusty's wheels touched. Five seconds

after that Curly touched. Two more seconds and Biff Bolton fish-tailed and settled. Together they taxied up to the line, cut their engines and legged out.

"I'll take mine later, Biff," Dusty grinned at the big pilot, as they grouped together and fished for cigarettes. "On second thought, I'll buy for the two of you. You did real well. In ten or fifteen more years I'll be proud of you, so help me."

Curly winked at Bolton.

3

"Something he ate, probably," he grunted. "I taught the tramp all he knows, and he's still breaking my heart."

Biff nodded solemnly.

"Yeah, I understand. But he does seem to handle the stick fair, in spots. He—ouch!"

Dusty put out a comforting hand.

"Sorry, Biff! Were you under my foot?"

The big pilot glared at him, crooked his right leg up and gingerly tested his foot with his left hand. Curly sighed with mock resignation.

"Forgive him, Biff," he said. "Air or ground—always getting in somebody's way. And the laugh is, that the government keeps right on paying him for it!"

Dusty smashed a clenched fist into the palm of the other hand.

"Thanks, Curly!" he exclaimed. "That reminds me. I'm clean and it's two weeks 'til payday. So—"

"So nothing!" Brooks cut in. "You go tap Major Drake this time. I'm not going to be a sucker all my life. You—"

"Switch off, mug! I was about to say that, in view of the fact that I could do with a little pin-money, I'm going to give you two bums a chance to prove how rotten you are. Now—"

He paused, fished a hand in his upper left tunic pocket and pulled out a crumpled five dollar bill. Brooks cursed as he saw it.

"And the guy says he's clean!"

"Oh, that!" snapped Dusty. "Just what your folks send me for keeping you out of trouble. But here's the idea. These crates, here, are triplets as regards speed. So it'll be up to the guy holding the stick, see? You, Biff, fly three hundred south and back. You, Curly, fly three hundred west, and back. And I'll buzz on the same east and back.

"Sergeant Trask can hold the watch on the three of us. It'll be from the time the wheels clear until they touch again. Fortunately, all the ships are fitted with air-mile distance recorders, so you guys will have to be honest for once. The winner gets the fifteen smackers. O.K.?"

"Sure!" grunted Biff. "Know just how I'm going to spend it!"

"Like hell you'll spend money I win!" snorted Curly. "Come onset's go! Hey, Sergeant Trask! Here a minute, will you?"

"Hold it there, wise boy!" Dusty yelled, putting out his hand and rubbing the thumb and forefinger together. "Cough up the five! Cough up the five—both of you! Trask can hold the dough!"

FIVE MINUTES later, Biff, who had won the take-off toss, sent his ship rocketing down the runway, pulled it clear and went flashing away to the south. Hardly had the thunder of his engine lost itself to the echo, than Curly Brooks tore into the air and faded out of sight to the west. And then Dusty rammed his throttle all the way home and sent his X ship streaking off toward the east.

Holding the craft at a five hundred foot altitude, he crouched forward over the stick, and maintained an alert watch for any other planes that might suddenly appear in his path. The airspeed ground-speed dial needle was quivering at the 715 m.p.h. mark, and at that speed split second movement of the controls, and their instantaneous response, was absolutely necessary.

But as he tore straight east from the Springfield, Massachusetts drome and went roaring out over Boston Harbor, not a plane of any design lumbered across his path. Nosing down to within a hundred feet of the rolling waters of the Atlantic, he leveled off and streaked on, one eye glued to the water ahead and the other to the instrument board.

In due time three hundred miles of air had rushed past his tapered wing, and he was in the act of zooming up in a loop to roll off and go thundering back, when suddenly the red signal light on the radio panel blinked rapidly. He glanced at it, scowled heavily.

"Some local call, probably," he grunted. "The hell with it! I need the ten bucks!"

The last had hardly left his lips, when he realized that a station was calling on the S.O.S. emergency wave-length. That was decidedly different!

Holding the plane in its terrific rush skyward, he snapped out his free hand, flipped on radio contact and twisted the dial knob to the S.O.S. reading. Instantly, excited words rattled out of the earphones.

"... for AT-Twelve! Heading for AT-Twelve! Send escort! Send escort! Send escort to AT-Twelve! Cannot hold out much longer!"

Over and over again the message was repeated. But the voice became fainter and fainter until it was unintelligible whispering sound. Turning on full reception volume didn't help any. One of two things was failing rapidly—either the broadcaster's voice, or his transmitting unit.

All thought of the race and its ten dollar prize gone from his mind, Dusty bent over the directional-finder dial. It indicated that the signals were coming from a point about two hundred miles southeast of his present position, and a good four hundred miles off the New Jersey coast.

Even as he figured that, he was swinging over to transmission, and grabbing up the transmitter tube.

"Calling signals from AT-Twelve!" he shouted into the tube. "Calling for check-back! What's your course? And what's the matter?"

As far as a reply coming out of the earphones was concerned, he might just as well have hollered down a rain barrel. Even the whispering had died away into silence. He tried three more times without success, and then switched off the set.

"Maybe a damn navy crate in trouble," he grunted. "Guess we'll take a look though."

Straightening out his climb, he swung the ship around and put the nose on a dead-on compass course for AT-Twelve—an imaginary square of water far out on the Atlantic.

Giving the ship its head, he tried three or four more times to raise the AT-Twelve broadcaster, but without any success whatsoever. The earphones were as silent as the inside of a tomb at midnight.

But suddenly, when a hundred miles or so were behind him, the earphones gave forth a vibrating high-keyed tone that jerked him up straight in the seat. Too many times had he heard that sound coming out of the air, not to recognize it instantly. He had flown into an area that was being static-jammed against both short and long wave radio communication.

Realization set his heart pending with expectant excitement, and the blood dancing through his veins. Something was in the wind, that was a cinch. The call had been made in English, but it didn't take a million dollars' worth of intelligence to figure out that the static-jamming had all the earmarks of Black Invader work.

"Come on, old girl!" he grunted, rapping his free fist against the wide-open throttle. "Methinks there's dirty work a-brewing at the cross-roads. Let's amble!"

To gain a bit of additional speed he shoved the nose down a shade and held it there. The props, controlled by constant speed gears, spun over at maximum revs, but the wing slicing through the air set up an eerie wail that drifted faintly through the sealed cockpit cowling. But Dusty didn't even notice it. He kept his eyes glued on the cloud spotted expanse of sky far ahead. If mental calculations were correct, he would be over the AT-Twelve area in another fifteen minutes.

But only nine of those fifteen minutes had slipped past into history, when he saw it—a dot, skimming across the top fringe of a cloud bank off to his right, and perhaps ten or twelve thousand feet below. Instantly he swung that way and steepened his dive. The X-Diesel monoplane virtually ate up the air as it thundered down.

Presently the dot took on definite shape and outline and Dusty found himself staring at a stubby-winged amphibian. But what jerked a curse of surprise from his lips a split second

THE SILVER TYPHOON

later, was realization that the craft was of Black Invader design. As a matter of fact, wings, hull, tail sections and everything were painted an unmistakable jet black. And a moment or two later he was even able to see the Black Invader air force insignia painted on the nose of the hull!

"What the hell? Is that rat trying to pull—"

He didn't finish the rest.

At that moment the monoplane amphibian, with its double tractor-pusher power-plant mounted atop the center section of the wing, cut around in a vicious split-arc turn and went racing for a nearby cloud bank. But it was still a quarter of a mile away when three shadows came streaking down on it from above—three shadows that instantly became three fleet Black Invader Navy pontooned ships as Dusty snapped his eyes toward them. A split second later the nose of each ship spewed out twin streams of jetting flame that zipped down toward the amphibian racing for the clouds.

"Something's screwy! I never did like Navy crates, anyway!"

Unconsciously bellowing the words aloud, Dusty, thumped down on left rudder, tapped the stick over a bit, and went streaking toward the three Black Navy planes. He was almost on top of them before his presence was noted. And even then, he was more or less ignored. The three Black planes altered their course slightly, but immediately swung back in and sprayed burst after burst of hot steel at the fleeing amphibian.

"So, not a free fight, eh?" Dusty cracked aloud. "Well, that's what you think!"

Pulling the nose up, he zoomed vertically for a good five

hundred feet. Then over he whipped, and down like a streak of greased lightning. Steadying himself, he lined up the left hand Black in his sights, and jabbed the trigger trips forward.

The two guns cowled into the nose, and the two cowled into the leading edge of the wing on either side of the center section, spoke as one gun—and a Black Invader pilot probably never knew what struck him. His plane, including himself, virtually fell apart in mid-air, and went showering down into oblivion. ONE GLANCE was enough for Dusty. In fact there was no time for a second glance. From out of nowhere, more Black ships slammed down to play the same trick on him. That is, they started to play it, but that sixth sense, God-given to the born fighter, warned him in the nick of time. He didn't wait to cheek on the warning. He simply sliced out of his dive, barrel-rolled four times and then went thundering up and over.

Only when he was upside down did he take time out to look around. The sight was not particularly pleasant. Six Black planes, all of them Black navy jobs, were maneuvering around as their pilots tried to get into attack position. The amphibian, though, was nowhere to be seen. It had lost itself in the cloud bank.

"Six of you, huh?" grunted Dusty. "Just a nice workout, I admit. But, sorry, that amphibian has got me curious. Why pump steel at the boy-friend?"

Flipping over right side up, he skidded clear of a zooming Black, thumbed his nose at the pilot, and went streaking toward the cloud bank. The Blacks, however, had undoubtedly figured that out, for two of them came rushing up to cut Dusty off. Their guns spat flame and he heard fingers of steel drumming savagely against the armor-plated coating of the fuselage. A brand new ship, and some bum was marking it up with slugs, huh?

"Don't want to go home, eh?" Dusty snarled.

And with that he whipped over and down in a terrific burst of speed. The Black below was caught cold, and the frantic movements of the plane proved it. Over on its side it flopped, then doubled back savagely. But the Black was just about five-and-a-half years too late.

Dusty's four-gun attack smashed his glass cowling to shimmering powder, to say nothing of the black skull-capped head under it. For perhaps two seconds the plane shot forward. Then an invisible fist seemed to smash down on it, and the craft dropped like a ball of lead.

Before it had hardly started down, Dusty had pulled out and was again racing for the cloud bank He thundered into it and through into the clear, like a slashed knife going through soft butter.

For a moment only patches of blue sky and more cloud banks confronted him. But as he snapped his eyes to the west, he saw three planes milling around is a series of crazy circles. Two of them were Black Navy ships, but the third was the mysterious amphibian.

Split-arcing toward thorn, he banged the already wide open throttle and cursed the plane on to greater speed. The three ships were a good ten miles away, but even at the distance he could see that the pontooned jobs were striving to "box" the amphibian and send it careening down into oblivion.

Just why he was rushing to the aid of an enemy ship, he didn't know. Nor did he pause to figure it out. Something was haywire; no doubt of it. Perhaps, if he got that amphibian off by itself he might learn something—and, perhaps not. But right now there was a two-to-one scrap, and the pilot of the amphibian was getting all the worst of it.

Five, six, seven miles whipped past, and then, as though at a mutual signal, the two pontooned ships cut away from the amphibian and came streaking toward Dusty, all guns spewing jetting flame. He grinned, slid his thumbs up to the trigger trips.

"Wasting ammo, sweethearts!" he grunted. "And I think you're going to need it. Now watch papa closely!"

Pulling back the stick he sent the X-Diesel rocketing heavenward. Below and ahead he could see the two pontooned ships following him up. One thousand feet higher he pulled the plane over on its back, and hung there for the fraction of a second. It was enough. The Blacks, thinking, obviously, that he was going to slide down the back side to complete the loop, split apart to be ready to swing back in for a perfect "box" attack. But they thought wrong.

Letting the nose drop just a shade, to gain maximum speed, Dusty shoved the stick up against the instrument board, held the rudder steady, and sent the plane swinging up and over in a three quarter outside loop. The result was that the two Blacks were left flat, racing back toward each other, and Dusty thundering down from above. It was so simple that he only used the two guns cowled into the engine. And even one of them would have been enough. The Black below him, and on the left, took his blazing burst without moving a muscle. And after that he couldn't; stone dead, he slumped forward against the stick, and the plane, engine wide open, tore down into wet oblivion below.

The other Black made a weak feint at hanging on his prop, and belted a burst or two at Dusty as he whipped past. But the Yank ace was ready for that. He skidded broadside to the left, let the plane flop into a power spin, then pulled it out and came screaming up. But by then the Black had probably realized his mistake for even as Dusty started to jab the trigger trips forward, the pontooned ship practically fell into a barrel roll and went tearing for the nearest cloud bank.

With a curse, Dusty started racing after him. Then suddenly he changed his mind and split-arced back east.

"A break for you, tramp!" he flung at the fleeing Black. "I'm still curious about that damn amphibian!"

FAR AHEAD of him he could see it, hugging every available cloud bank, twin props clawing air at maximum revs. A glance at the directional compass on the instrument board brought a puzzled frown to Dusty's brows. If the amphibian held its 'present' course, it would eventually smack the lower end of New Jersey right on the nose.

Tearing after it, he absently mulled over a hundred-and-one different reasons for the presence of a Black amphibian so close to the American coast. Was it a Black spy trying to slip in, the attack of the other ships being merely a fake? Was the pilot some Yank who had escaped from Black Navy ships patrolling the middle Atlantic? Was it a Black who had proved traitor, and was fleeing the revenge of his countrymen?

Those and countless more questions raced across Dusty's brain as he tore after the other ship. And to all, the answer was the same—he didn't know, but he was damn well going to find out.

On impulse he reached out and snapped on radio contact, and spun the dial to the S.O.S. reading.

"Amphibian ahead! Amphib—"

He cut off the rest as the familiar static-jamming sound poured out of the earphones. For the time being, anyway, the radio was out.

"Okay, then!" he grunted, snapping off the set. "We'll just go where you go!"

Hunching forward over the stick he concentrated on catching up with the amphibian. That took about fifteen minutes, and by then the eastern coast of New Jersey was a dark line far down on the horizon.

On the alert for any tricks, Dusty closed in cautiously. The amphib was a four-place job, and he had noted the rear gunner's compartment aft of the wing. But the twin guns sticking out through the swivel-vent did not move, and as he slid in closer he was able to see that the compartment was empty, as far as a rear gunner was concerned.

That fact certain in his mind, he throttled a bit, cut off to the side, and then swung back in so that he was flying wing to wing with the Black craft. Countless holes were in its single wing, the hull was grooved and marked where steel bullets had struck and glanced off, and the glass cowling of the hull cockpit was but a splintered shambles.

All that he noted in a glance, then riveted his eyes on the hunched over figure in the pit. The man wore the uniform of the Black Invaders; even the black skull cap that draped down over the nape of his neck.

Rigid, Dusty stared popeyed at the man who was looking straight ahead. And then, suddenly, the figure turned toward him, started visibly, then half raised his free hand in a gesture that could mean most anything.

Dusty hardly noticed the gesture. It was the face that held his eyes like a powerful magnet. The left side was smeared with blood, but even that did not conceal the hawk-like nose, the wide-set and deep-sunken eyes, and the lean, pointed jaw of the typical Black Invader!

CHAPTER 2
SEALED LIPS

"BY GOD—DAMNED if he isn't a Black!" Dusty's mumbled exclamation echoed back to him faintly as he peered hard across the narrow strip of air space separating the two ships. One of his questions was answered. The pilot of the amphibian was a Black Invader, but—so what? Why had he been attacked by his own men? And, perhaps more important, why in hell was he now flying full out for the American coast?

As Dusty thought of the last, his face got hard, and the

corners of his mouth went down. Much as he hated Blacks, he hated more, a rat who would dash for the safety of enemy territory to escape the vengeance of his own comrades. And that certainly seemed to be the case right now.

At that moment the other pilot reached out his free hand, picked up the radio transmitter tube. Almost simultaneously, Dusty's red signal light blinked rapidly. But as he snapped on contact he heard the static-jamming noise in the earphones for the third time.

Unconsciously, he shook his head and gestured with his free hand. The pilot of the amphibian nodded, and although Dusty wasn't sure, he thought he saw blood flecked lips twist back in a bitter smile. And at the same time the amphibian nosed down a bit and increased its speed toward shore.

"Easy!" shouted Dusty. "Any funny work and I'll—"

He cut off the rest with a puzzled grunt. The other pilot, as though he had actually heard Dusty's words was weakly waving a "come on" signal with his free hand. The exertion seemed to be too much for the man. His body slumped forward against the Dep control wheel of the craft, and it went plunging down, almost at the vertical.

Unable to do a thing about it, Dusty watched the craft hurtle down toward the rolling waters below. But when it was little more than a couple of thousand feet above their foamy, white-capped crests, the nose of the amphib arced slowly up until the plane was on even keel once more.

Diving down, Dusty swung in alongside again, and continued his frowning scrutiny of the strange figure under the shat-

tered cowl. But the other did not return his gaze any more. Face toward the shore, the man sat like a statue of marble. Better, like a dead pilot frozen to the controls of his plane.

He didn't seem to move a muscle until the craft was less than two hundred yards from a sandy beached strip of shoreline. Then he moved his left hand, reached for the throttle. A second or two later the spinning props slackened to idling speed, and the plane slanted into a long flat glide.

Fifty yards from the shore Dusty saw the wheels slide down out of the hull. He had already cut his own engine, and was guiding his plane automatically as he kept his eyes on the other.

"If you're thinking of fooling me," he muttered aloud, "letting me sit down first, and then you zoom off—just forget it! You haven't seen half of what I can do with this crate!"

But the next few seconds made it plainly evident that the strange pilot had no such idea in mind. The amphibian lost altitude rapidly, wobbled dangerously a couple of times, and then flopped down on the smooth and hard-packed sand like a tired bird.

At practically the same instant, Dusty touched, some ninety yards up the beach. Wheel braking just enough, he skidded the ship around and taxied toward the amphibian. Fifteen yards from it, he full-braked, snapped open the glass cowl and leaped out.

Even as his feet touched the sand, he was pulling his service automatic from its holster. Training the gun on the motionless figure now slumped over to one side in the cockpit, he ran over to the amphib and climbed up on the hull.

"Just hold the pose, fella!" he grunted, sticking his head, and the gun, in through the shattered cowing. "And if you don't savvy English, just keep your lamps on this gun. Now—"

"Don't—be a—fool! I'm—Yank! I—I—"

THE WEAK, moaning voice trailed off into a husky whisper. In a flash Dusty bolstered his gun, and climbed down into the cockpit. He put an arm around the man, eased him up to a more comfortable position. Pulling out a handkerchief with his other hand he dabbed it gently on the jagged gash that stretched from the man's left eye to his left ear. As he did, he also noticed a dull red stain on the man's left side, just below the armpit.

"Easy, buzzard," he said quietly. "My mistake. I didn't know. You look like a—"

"Never mind!" came the wheezing words off the blood-flecked lips. "Don't blame you. Listen—listen—must reach X-Thirty-four! X—X-Thirty-four!"

A violent coughing spell stopped all further effort. Dusty let the man lean against him to ease the strain; waiting in frowning silence. X-34? Hell that was the code number of General Horner, chief of U.S. Intelligence!

With a pitiful but valiant effort, the wounded man regained control of his speech.

"Tried to make—Washington!" he mumbled. "Couldn't— Blacks tried—tried to head me off! Got me—damn them! Only—three hundred—to go—and they got—me! Must get word to—X-Thirty-four!"

"Sure, sure!" said Dusty. "I'll take you there, pronto. Now, put your right arm around me, and I'll move you out of the seat. It—"

The other's head wobbled from side to side.

"No—no use! I'm finished. But you—you must get to—X-Thirty-four! Tell him—tell—tell—"

The words died out and the eyes fluttered closed. The man's body relaxed and slumped against Dusty like a dead weight. He gripped the man's good shoulder, squeezed it just a bit.

"Hang on, hang on!" he shouted. "You're going to come through—you're going to! What shall we tell X-Thirty-four?"

The lids fluttered up, but dazed, glassy orbs stared into Dusty's face. The man tried to laugh, but it was only a rasping cough.

"Go to hell—Mlada! Damn your—black heart! I'd rot in hell—hell—before I'd—! Go—ahead—kill me! Go ahead—ahead—ahead!"

Mlada? The strange name meant nothing to Dusty. He stared helplessly at the delirious man; shook him gently.

"X-Thirty four," he shouted. "What about X-Thirty-four?"

For a second the other's eyes cleared just a bit. He started violently, winced, and the bloody features of his face twisted with excruciating pain.

"Yes—yes!" he gasped. "X-Thirty-four! Tell him that Sixteen didn't die! I wasn't killed. They—held me prisoner. Mlada—held me prisoner. But—I saw—I saw! Tell him—Mlada—St. Albans—it's there—they—they—have—"

The effort was too much. The man struggled for words, but his breath only whistled eerily between clenched teeth. Dusty could almost feel the grim reaper reaching out for the man, and instinctively clasped his other arm about him.

"Come back, Sixteen!" he shouted wildly. "Come back! You must tell me more. St. Albans—where? What about Mlada? Come back, Sixteen!"

The man spoke again, but he didn't open his eyes. Limp and virtually lifeless, he moved only his lips.

"St. Albans—England!" he choked. "Escaped—got away in—this. But—Mlada—he found out—damn his soul! Must have radioed—Black Navy—ships! Thanks—thanks for coming! But—Mlada—knows I—saw! Tell X-Thirty-four—Washington Intelligence! Tell him—Sixteen saw—at St. Albans! I did—I did see—I did—"

"Saw what?" yelled Dusty desperately as the other's voice trailed off. "What did you see?"

The man groaned, raised his left hand, turned it palm upward. With his other hand he pointed at three little dots—purple, like tattoo ink—marked in the crease of the middle joint of the little finger.

"Tell X-Thirty-four—about that!" he whispered. "He'll know—it's Sixteen! Tell him—that—that I saw—saw—"

The man's body suddenly twitched violently. A sharp, rasping cry spilled off his lips. He arched his back, clawed frantically at thin air with blood-smeared fingers. And then, like a deflated balloon, he seemed to fold up and go completely limp. But for Dusty's arms around him, the man would have toppled over against the instrument board.

"Steady, Sixteen!"

But words were useless, now. Sixteen, or whoever he was, had passed beyond the realm of spoken words. He was dead.

For a moment or two Dusty sat holding the man, brain spinning over with memory of the jerky, disconnected phrases that spilled from the man's lips. St. Albans—England—Mlada? What the hell was it all about? Obviously the man had escaped, stolen the amphibian and flown the Atlantic.

By way of confirming that thought, Dusty twisted to the side, peered at the fuel gauge on the instrument board. It showed that there was enough fuel for six or seven hundred mare miles left in tanks which, when full, would permit a three thousand mile cruising radius for the plane. Yup, the dead man had probably flown the Atlantic from some place in Europe—St. Albans, England, if what he had said meant anything.

He cut off his thought, eased the dead body back into the seat, stood up.

"Okay, buzzard," he murmured. "I'll take your message to Horner. Maybe he'll be able to carry on from there."

He let the rest trail off, stared down at the man. A Yank—a Yank agent? Hell, if anyone ever looked like a real Black Invader, this man did! Yet, his English had been perfect.

Dusty cursed, climbed out of the amphibian.

"Do your thinking later, sap!" he growled at himself. "Yes or no, Horner should learn of this anyway. Sixteen? Damned if I haven't heard Jack Horner speak of that number!"

He was in the act of legging into his ship, when he suddenly heard footsteps pounding the hard sand behind him. He turned around, saw a Yank infantry, soldier running toward him. The soldier skidded to a halt, clicked his heels and saluted with his rifle.

"Saw you land, sir," he panted. "Can I help?"

Dusty shoved his half drawn automatic back into its holster and nodded.

"Right," he said, pointing toward the amphibian. "You can stand guard on that—"

The rest he left hanging in mid-air. The soldier had snapped up his rifle, and the muzzle was not more than six inches from Dusty's chest.

"What the—?"

"Just stand still!" the other snapped.

Like a snake his hand shot out and jerked Dusty's automatic free. Substituting it for the rifle, he trained it on him.

"Now my friend," he sneered, the corners of his mouth sagging down. "You will walk over to that plane—and be very careful! I'd hate to shoot you with your own gun!"

DUSTY DIDN'T move a muscle but he was boiling with rage inside. At first glance the man had looked like any one of millions of American infantrymen. But now he could see the difference. No more than just the expression in the eyes—but, their cruel, smoldering glint was quite, sufficient.

Steeling himself, he forced a grin to his lips.

"Very neat," he said. "I suppose you just happened to be passing by, eh?"

The other returned his smile.

"Not exactly," he said. "But we've been expecting your friend for several hours."

He stopped long enough to jerk his head toward the amphibian.

"Expecting him," he said, "unless we received word that he had been—er—detained. Now kindly walk ahead of me!"

Still Dusty didn't move. Eyes clamped on the man, he widened his grin, and tried a stall for time. If this rat had seen him land, maybe some real Americans had also seen him.

"Why walk over there?" he grunted. "The pilot's dead."

The other stiffened, and his eyes narrowed. With a quick movement he stepped around in back of Dusty and pressed the gun muzzle against the small of his back. There followed a few seconds of silence. Then the man spoke again; returned to a position in front of Dusty.

"Yes," he nodded. "I can see that he is quite dead. That is fortunate, and unfortunate. There is no need to take you both. But you will have to speak for him. He talked before he died."

The Black agent leaned forward, gimlet eyes boring Dusty's face. The Yank shrugged.

"So what?"

"So it will be well for you to tell me what he said!" the words were shot right back.

Dusty furrowed his brows as though he were in deep thought. And without appearing to do so, he snapped a glance down the beach. But no welcome sight of figures running toward him greeted him—just flat hard sand slanting down into the surf.

"What did he say?"

The words smacked against Dusty's eardrums like machine-gun fire. He returned the man's agate stare. Then suddenly relaxed.

"Hold the trigger," he said. "I'll tell you. It wasn't much—damned if I understand it. He couldn't talk very well. But he seemed to say something about the hull of the ship. About something he'd hidden there—there, in the nose."

As Dusty spoke, he braced himself inwardly and pointed at the amphibian with his right hand. The Black started to turn, checked the movement. But he checked it about one millionth of a second too late.

Like a sledgehammer Dusty's clenched fist shot down, and smacked the man's gun wrist. The man yelped with pain, and the gun barked sound, but the bullet tore through the skirt of Dusty's tunic and buried itself in the sand in back.

No second shot was fired. The automatic slipped from the man's paralyzed fingers. But before it had started to drop Dusty had crashed over his left, virtually sunk it in the side of the man's neck. What the first blow did to the man's hand the second did to his whole body. Stiff as a board he fell over backward and hit the sand flat on his back.

In one continued movement Dusty scooped up his own automatic, and the Black's rifle. The rifle he swung over his head and flung it far out into the surf. Then reaching down with his left hand he hooked his fingers in the Black's collar, jerked him to his feet and shook him so hard that the man's teeth clicked like castanets.

"Now I'll pitch for awhile!" he grated. "How come you're here? Any more of your pack around?"

The Black glared sullenly, and kept his lips pressed tightly together.

"Long time no talk, eh?" Dusty snapped. "Okay! We'll try another way!"

As he spoke the words he slapped the muzzle of his automatic down the man's left cheek. The skin split like melon peel, and the man screamed with pain.

"Open up! Who sent you here? And from where?"

The other's fear-glazed eyes fastened on the upraised automatic. He cringed, tried to put up a protecting hand. Dusty clipped him on the wrist, and the hand dropped.

"No, no!" howled the Black. "Orders come! Orders come to me at—"

Crack!

A rifle shot from ahead and to the right! The Black's body twitched, his lips curled back in a funny little smile, and his eyes went blank.

Crack!

Sand flew up at Dusty's feet. He didn't see it, only felt it. He was already in motion. Letting go the Black, who immediately fell over and lay still, he leaped back and under the wing of his ship.

Crack!

Something twanged off the engine cowling and went whining off into oblivion. Dusty hesitated a split second, shot a glance in the direction of the sound but could only see mass after mass of tangled surf grass. He thought a section of it moved, but he didn't wait to make sure. In one leap he hurled himself into the cockpit. Hardly settled in the seat, he slammed on left wheel brake, swung the plane around and opened up the throttle. Above the roar of his engine he heard two more rifle shots, heard also the steel-nosed bullets as they slapped through the rudder, not over a foot back of his hand. And then he pulled the wheels clear and zoomed up into the air.

ONE HUNDRED feet up, he slammed the ship over and around, and came tearing back. He caught a flash picture of the lifeless figure on the sand, a few yards from the deserted amphibian. Then he snapped his eyes ahead and to the right. A figure was racing madly through surf grass that came up to his waist, toward a car parked on a beach road some hundred yards from the shore.

Suddenly he stopped, spun around and flung up his rifle. It was then that Dusty saw the cruel, hate-twisted face. The figure was garbed in civilian clothes. Then the rifle spat flame and a hole appeared in the right wing. Nosing down, Dusty slid his fingers up to the trigger trips.

"His side-kick, eh?" he grunted. "Well, damn you, join him!"

Two of Dusty's guns snarled sound. The figure in the surf grass flung up both his hands, and his rifle went arcing off as he went over like a ten-pin. Just a short burst of five slugs that drilled right through the man's chest.

The instant they had sped on their way, Dusty pulled back on the stick and sent his ship thundering up for altitude. At fifteen thousand he leveled off, and headed straight for the Washington military field. It would be only a matter of minutes, but nevertheless he decided to contact General Horner by air.

So, snapping on radio contact and spinning the dial, he called official Intelligence H.Q. The check-back came through instantly.

"Intelligence H.Q. Go ahead!"

"A-Six calling!" Dusty replied. "Important that I see X-Thirty-four. Coming into the Washington field now. Will report to his office immediately."

"Sorry, A-Six," the earphones crackled back. "But X-Thirty-four is not here."

"Where is he?" Dusty asked. "It's important!"

"Sorry! Can't give that information over the air. Suggest you report in to Major Jordon!"

Dusty cursed, and snapped off the set without bothering to thank the man at the other end. He knew Jordon well—officer in charge of signal communications, and one of General Horner's right-hand men. Jordon would know where the general was, all right.

Cutting the throttle he went sliding down toward Washington military field, now directly ahead and below. A couple of greaseball non-coms came running out as he taxied up to the line. They'd seen him often before, and both grinned recognition.

"Guess you're expecting the car, huh, skipper?" one of them asked as Dusty legged out.

The ace nodded.

"Yeah. Getting to be a habit, isn't it?"

"Got General Horner's orders 'bout two minutes ago," the non-com said. "So the car's coming."

"General Horner's orders?" echoed Dusty sharply. "He sent orders through for me?"

The greaseball gulped, looked surprised.

"Yeah, sure, sir! Not more than three minutes ago. Said that a car was on its way. It—guess that's it now, skipper."

The man pointed up the tarmac at a low-slung staff car rolling toward them. Dusty scowled at it, started to speak, but checked himself and stood waiting as the car came to a stop in front of him. A staff sergeant behind the wheel climbed out and saluted.

"Captain Ayres, sir?"

"Right," Dusty replied quietly. "You're from General Horner?"

"Yes sir. He said you were coming in here. Sent me down to get you."

Dusty grinned and climbed in back.

"Darn nice of the general, service like this," he said. "O.K., let's go. Oh, corporal, fuel her up will you?"

The non-com's reply was drowned out as the sergeant driver meshed gears and the car rolled away. A crooked smile on his lips, Dusty leaned forward.

"I understood that General Horner wasn't at his office, sergeant," he said.

The driver spoke without turning.

"Isn't, sir. At the Research Bureau. Your message was phoned through. And he sent me down to get you."

"Oh, I see," grunted Dusty, and leaned back.

Through half-closed lids he watched the buildings sliding by on both sides, unconsciously braced himself as the driver turned corners without slackening speed very much. Then presently he leaned forward again.

"Oh, sergeant?"

"Yes sir?"

"Take the second on the left!" grunted Dusty.

The driver flicked his head around, turned instantly front again.

"But that's not the way to the Research Building, sir," he said.

"I know that," said Dusty. "It's the way to the War Department Buildings—and that's where we're going!"

"But, sir, General—"

"Yes, yes, that's very nice," Dusty cut in. Then in hard tones, "You rats are getting cruder as the war goes on! The War Department Building, and no fooling, you! I've got a nice little slug all set to slap into the back of your thick skull. So keep both hands on the wheel!"

The driver stiffened, turned his head. Dusty let him see the automatic he held in his hand.

"Like I said, bum!" he grated. "A nice little slug that'll hurt like hell! Now, second the right!"

The other turned front again, hunched stiffly over the wheel. Gun trained on him, Dusty leaned back against the cushions. A few seconds later the driver slowed down for the turn. Dusty grinned. But it faded from his face instantly and he let out a wild yell and flung himself to the floor of the car. The driver had thumped down on the accelerator, and the car was roaring full speed diagonally across the street toward a building front.

In a matter of split seconds there was the sound of a terrific crash. An unseen hand grabbed hold of Dusty, lifted him up and then smashed him down again. A thousand lights exploded before his eyes. He had the crazy sensation of spinning head over heels through crimson flames. And then the sky fell down on top of him.

CHAPTER 3
SATAN'S DOUBLE

WHEN HE again opened his eyes, he found himself sitting on the sidewalk, back against a stone building wall, and gaping foolishly into the moon-shaped face of a District of Columbia policeman.

Beyond the policemen was a crowd of people, half military and half civilian. Two other policemen were keeping them back from a heap of junk half buried in the building wall. Absently, Dusty realized it was what was left of the staff car. Then he saw a still form on the sidewalk, over which a policeman's coat had been hastily thrown. And then he heard in the distance, the wail of an ambulance siren.

The sound pierced his brain, brought memory back, and steadied his jangling nerves.

"I'm all right," he grumbled. "Give me a hand, officer."

"Better take it easy, captain. Sure you're not hurt?"

Dusty's left side felt as though it had stopped a twelve-inch naval shell, but he shook his head, grabbed the policeman's arm for support and pulled himself to his feet.

"Nope," he said. "Lucky I guess. Just let me get my breath, and then I'll borrow that radio patrol car I see at the curb."

"Yes sir," the policeman said mechanically. "But what happened, sir? Your driver—he's dead."

Dusty looked down at the covered over figure on the sidewalk.

"Now ain't that too bad!" he grunted. "But he'll have company where he's gone."

The policeman stared at him.

"Huh?" he ejaculated. Then scowling, "Just because he isn't an officer, captain, is no—"

Dusty cut him off with a gesture.

"That man would love to slit your throat if he were alive," he said. "And do you know why?"

The other backed up a step, peered at Dusty with half closed, doubt-filled eyes.

"Slit my throat? Why?"

Dusty tapped him on his broad chest.

"Because you're an American," he said. "Now figure that out and you'll have plenty to tell the little woman when you go off duty. Meantime, I'm borrowing the patrol car. You'll find it parked in front of the War Department Building. The name is Captain Ayres, air force. His—you'll have to ask Fire-Eyes!"

Leaving the policeman dumbfounded and rooted in his tracks, Dusty shouldered through the mob that shouted a million different questions at him, and climbed into the patrol car.

FIVE MINUTES later he slid into the curb at the War Department Building and climbed out. Running up the long

flight of stone steps, he shoved through the big swinging doors and went over to the elevator line.

A couple of staff flunkies, walking past, stopped short and stared at him in amazement. It was only then that he realized that he was not exactly presentable for parade-ground inspection. The left side of his tunic was in shreds. His hat was gone completely and the left knee of his breeches was hanging down over the top of his field-boot. The parts of his uniform that weren't ripped and torn were smeared with grease and street dust. His hands and face were grimy.

"Good heavens!" gasped one of the flunkies. "Did you meet with an accident?"

"Nope," grinned Dusty stepping into an elevator. "The accident met with me. Fifty-eight, chief, and snappy!"

The last was for the operator, who immediately slammed the doors shut and sent the car rocketing upward. On the fifty-eighth floor Dusty stepped off and went over to a staff major seated behind a desk at the beginning of a long corridor. The man's eyes popped, and he half rose from his chair as Dusty approached.

"My God! What—"

"Nothing," Dusty cut him off. "Where is General Horner?"

"Oh, you're Ayres, aren't you," the other said, as his eyes lighted up with recognition. "I took your call. Did you see Major Jordon?"

"No. But I want to see General Horner."

"I'm sorry, but I do not know where he is. You'll have to see

Major Jordon. He's in the General's office now. But your uniform, captain! It's not exactly—er—"

Dusty didn't wait for him to finish it. With a nod he started down the long corridor, turned into the one that led off at right angles at the end, and headed for a door upon which was the lettering:

General J.T. Horner
PRIVATE

He went up to it, grasped the knob and started to twist when suddenly a sharp noise stopped him.

"P-s-s-s-t!"

Glancing down the corridor he saw the figure of a man in the uniform of a staff corporal beckoning to him. The man was standing half in and half out of an open doorway. The light from a window in back of the man blurred out the features of his face. Hesitating a second, Dusty released his grasp on the door knob and walked toward him.

"What's the idea?" he grunted, peering hard at the man's face which he now saw clearly.

It was quite ordinary—oval-shaped, a chubby complexion, and a trick mustache.

"Excuse me, Captain Ayres," said the man, just the faint trace of an Irish brogue in his voice, "but I'd like to talk to you a minute, if it's all the same to you, sir."

The man jerked his head toward the room. Dusty glanced in, saw that it was a file-room, and deserted. Moving his right hand closer to his holstered automatic he nodded.

"Okay! After you, soldier."

The other grinned, stepped into the room and sat down in a chair. Dusty closed the door, leaned his back against it.

"Well?" he grunted. "What's it all about?"

And then, to his amusement, the soldier chuckled.

"Guess I haven't lost my touch if I fooled you, kid!"

Had the roof fallen in at that moment Dusty wouldn't have noticed it. Jaw sagging, eyes sticking out like marbles on the end of two sticks, he gaped at the soldier.

"What—my God—you—you Jack?"

Jack Horner, known to a select few as Agent 10, got to his feet and walked over, hand outstretched.

"Right the first guess," he grinned. "But what the devil has happened to you?"

Dusty ignored the question. His eyes were still popping. The figure in front of him looked like most anyone except Jack Horner.

"Never mind about me," he grunted. "I thought you were still in hospital, convalescing from that knife wound in your back? What's the idea?"

"Entirely mine," the other replied. "The general insisted that I stay there, but I managed to talk him into letting me help around here. Was going damn near crazy. As a matter of fact I wanted to get back into harness, but we compromised on this job for a week or so. And a blasted job it is, too."

"Yeah?" echoed Dusty, gesturing with his hand. "What's it all about? Why the get-up?"

Agent 10 grimaced.

"The general is trying to crack down on the Black agent ring in Washington," he said. "I'm supposed to be a file clerk, but I'm really checking the record of every man in the department. The general thought it best to start from here. God, I'm fed up to the teeth, and it's only my third day on the blasted job. Now what about you? Crashed?"

Dusty had forgotten his own experiences for the moment, due to the surprise of meeting his old pal. But it all came back to him in a rush, and he stiffened.

"What did Agent Sixteen look like, Jack?" he asked suddenly.

It was Jack Horner's turn to stiffen.

"Agent Sixteen?" he gasped. "What about him? He was caught and killed by the Blacks just after the fall of Paris. About the best man we had in Europe, too."

"You saw him killed?" Dusty asked.

"Why, no, but he was. I'm sure of it. But, say, what the devil are you driving at?"

Dusty shrugged, took hold of young Horner's arm and led him over to the opposite side of the room from the door.

"Listen, Jack," he said in a half whispered voice, "something damn screwy happened today."

And then in crisp, right-to-the-point sentences he outlined everything to his friend.

"What it all adds up to mean," he finished, "damned if I can figure, exactly. But the Blacks are scared stiff that he might have told me something really tangible. Hence the rat popping upon the beach. And that staff car driver, too. As a matter of fact, that was just a hunch I had—a hunch that your Dad would have met me instead of sending a car. So I tried the bluff on the driver—and clicked. Somehow, the bums must have listened in when I called Intelligence H.Q. A Black agent ring in Washington is right! Bet the tramps even know what I eat for breakfast!"

HE CHUCKLED as he spoke the last. But there was no responding chuckle from Agent 10's lips. Face grave brows furrowed the man simply eyed Dusty in silence. Then he slowly sucked in his breath.

"I can hardly believe it!" he breathed. "But it must have been Sixteen. Under normal conditions he even looked more like a Black than they do themselves—though he was all Yank from head to foot. And those dots on his little finger—an old system we used to use. Abandoned it a good six months before war broke out. So it wouldn't have gained the Blacks a thing to copy it—doubt if they even knew about it. It must have been Sixteen—good God!"

"Yeah, me too!" grunted Dusty. "But what's this Mlada? Is he a Black, or what?"

"Worse!" young Horner replied savagely, "He's fourteen different kinds of a devil moulded together in human form. Hell, even Fire-Eyes himself is big-hearted Elmer compared with Mlada. The man lives only to slaughter. He's in complete charge of the rehabilitation forces. Rather, head clean-up man, you might say."

"Meaning what?" frowned Dusty. "I don't exactly get you."

"Fire-Eyes conquers," Agent 10 answered, "and Mlada sees

39

that the victims say conquered. He crushes uprisings and re-
bellions of the peoples of captured countries—and does it with
a ruthlessness and utter disregard for life that even you, in spite
of what you've already seen, could never imagine. So he's at St.
Albans, eh? I've been wondering where the devil has been
keeping himself. God, would I enjoy killing that hellhound!"

"Just why St. Albans?" asked Dusty. "I know the place—a
small town about twenty miles north of London, on the Lon-
don-Midland railroad. Been there lots of times, but never noticed
anything particularly outstanding about it. Hendon was a hell
of a sight more interesting from the aeronautical point of view."

"Yes, I know," Agent 10 nodded, "but that was before the
Blacks started smashing the world. Hendon was laid flat during
the attack on London. The last I heard, St Albans was Black
European H.Q. But—it must be more than that now. Are you
sure that Sixteen didn't say anything else—anything about what
he saw? Maybe, just a word, that perhaps you've forgotten?
Think hard, kid. It might mean everything!"

But Dusty simply shook his head.

"He didn't get that far, Jack," he said. "I'm positive of it,
absolutely."

The faint ray of hope that had come into young Horner's
face faded out, and he stared dully at the opposite wall. Dusty
tugged at his lower lip a moment and cursed softly.

"I think our first move, Jack, is to lay all the facts before your
dad," he said. By the way, where in hell is he?"

"Officially, he's supposed to have gone up to Boston for a
conference with Northeastern Area H.Q.," the other replied.

"Come on, we'll borrow a ship at the field, and you can fly us to where he really is. Act as though you'd taken me on as temporary orderly, or something."

"Okey," nodded Dusty as they started for the door. "But is there something in the wind—all this mystery about where the general is, I mean?"

Young Horner hesitated, half shrugged.

"Perhaps," he said. "Perhaps soon we'll be able to go Black Invader inventions one better. Now just keep your shirt on. And remember, I'm your orderly, or any other damn thing you want me to be. Here, sir, allow me to open the door."

As the Intelligence man flung open the door, Dusty stalked out into the hall, whirled around.

"I don't care how busy you are, soldier!" he said in a loud voice. "If you can't tell me where General Horner is, you can at least show me to the uniform stores! Damned if I'm going to wear this wreck any longer and I haven't time to go back to my field!"

As he poured out the words, he started inwardly. A blurred figure at the far end of the hall had suddenly slipped around the L corner and disappeared. The sudden glint in Agent 10's eyes told Dusty that his pal had not missed the movement either. Then young Horner saluted smartly.

"Yes, captain," he said. "The stores building is over on J Street. I'll take you there, sir."

Walking stiffly ahead of Dusty, Agent 10 went down the hall, and turned left into the elevator corridor. As they approached the desk, the staff major, still seated behind it, gave them both a sharp glance, and finally fastened his eyes on Dusty.

"You saw Major Jordon, captain?" he asked.

"He was too busy, sir," Dusty replied without stopping. "But, I'll be back. Going over to stores now and get out of these things. Borrowing this man to help me out."

Before the staff major could say anything they both stepped into a waiting elevator and shot downward in silence. Out at the curb, Agent 10 signaled one of the several waiting staff cars. As the first one rolled up, he jerked his head at the driver.

"The captain wants me to drive, soldier," he grunted. "I'll bring it back."

The driver hesitated, glanced at Dusty, and at the pilot's nod, shrugged and slid out from behind the wheel. Young Horner took his place and held the door open for Dusty.

"All right, sir," he said. "We'll be at stores in five minutes."

The car had traveled but a couple of blocks when Dusty tapped his pal on the arm.

"How about me taking that wheel, kid? Maybe I can make it a shade faster. You're just out of hospital, you know."

The Intelligence man cursed angrily.

"One more crack about me and that damn place!" he snapped. "And I'll let you have it right on the button! This is my show, so pipe down!"

Dusty grinned and leaned back.

"Such language to an officer!" he murmured. "But then, you and Curly never did show respect to your—hey! You're going in the opposite direction to the field!"

Agent 10's immediate answer was to increase the speed of the car and go tearing around a corner on two wheels.

"Take a look back, dummy!" he grunted between clenched teeth.

Dusty turned in the seat and stared back through the rearview mirror. A second car was spinning around the corner they had just turned.

"Think they'd call it a day, just because they missed a couple of times?" Jack Horner's voice drifted into his ears. "Hang on! I'm going to shake 'em. Haven't got time to give them a scrap."

AND HANGING on occupied all of Dusty's attention for the next twenty minutes. Although Jack Horner was only a week or so out of the hospital, it certainly had no effect whatsoever on his driving ability. Accelerator clamped to the floor boards he sent the car spinning and twisting through the streets of Washington like something possessed.

For several miles the trailing car stuck like glue. But a hairpin turn by Jack Horner, just outside Georgetown, caused the other car to overshoot its mark. And three minutes after that the Intelligence man had lost it completely. Still twisting, turning, and doubling back, he finally shot the car onto the Washington Military field tarmac and braked it to an abrupt stop.

With a deep sigh, Dusty relaxed, wiped a hand across his forehead.

"Wow!" he husked. "Ten years of my life gone, just like that!"

"Just loafed along," his pal grinned. "Okay, let's get a cabin job. I once did you a favor, and you're giving me a joy-ride, see? My name's Walker."

It was simple for them to carry the bluff through, and in a matter of minutes Dusty was pulling a two-place cabin biplane clear of the field and swinging up into sunset-lighted skies. At fifteen thousand he leveled off, glanced at young Horner seated at his side.

"O.K.," he grunted. "Time to unmask. Where do we find your Dad?"

"Take a round-about course for Memphis," the other replied. "We're headed for T-Fourteen to be exact—about forty miles north of the city. But—"

He paused, glanced nervously out through the cabin windows.

"But be sure to make it a round-about course," he continued. "Those damn bums want you plenty bad!"

"Yeah, so it would seem," grinned Dusty. "And the hell of it is, they don't know that I don't know. But, come on, open up some more. I'm a curious bird, you know. What's your Dad doing at T-Fourteen? What the hell's there?"

The other made a face.

"Frankly, I don't know?" he said.

"Don't know?" echoed Dusty. "What is this—twenty questions and answers, or something?"

"Just about," Jack Horner nodded. "Naturally, for obvious reasons, the general told me where he was going. He also told Jordon. We might have to contact him—just as you and I are doing, now. But why he went there—it was last night—I don't know. Except—"

"Yeah?" encouraged Dusty as he paused. "Except—?"

"Except that he hinted something about a new gadget we

hope to spring on the Blacks," the Intelligence man said slowly. "He wouldn't say anything definite, just hinted that something new and mighty valuable was in the making. Maybe, he'll tell us when we see him. And maybe he won't."

Dusty sighed, swung the plane up toward a billowing cloud bank.

Suddenly he bent forward and peered hard up at the cloud bank. A shadow was flitting about its top-most fringes. A shadow that split seconds later materialized into a Dart monoplane, streaking down at them and spitting twin streams of jetting flame from its pointed snout.

"Good God—look—a Black Dart!"

Agent 10's wild cry was just a waste of breath to Dusty. He was already slamming the cabin plane over on wing and sending it down in a wild power spin.

"Hold tight!" he bellowed above the thunder of the engine. "The clouds below are our only chance!"

CHAPTER 4
DEATH'S HOME TOWN

LEFT FOOT jammed down hard on the rudder pedal, both hands holding the stick hard against his stomach, Dusty held his breath in hellish suspense as the plane spun furiously for the clouds below. And meanwhile, from above, came the savage yammer of machine-gun fire, and the heart chilling echo of steel slugs smacking through the rear section of the fuselage. The cabin plane was equipped with a pair of

Brownings, but for the moment he didn't even give them a thought. In any other ship he would have slashed out of the spin and gone zooming back to give the unknown attacker a bit of his own medicine. But in this ship? Hell, it wasn't even as good as a training crate—just an aerial buzz-wagon for off-the-record joy-hops about the field.

To scrap a Black Dart with it would be just the same as asking for quarters six feet under the sod, with a granite slab on top. Yeah—he who quits the scrap and runs away, lives to scrap another day! Damn right!

"Can we make it?"

Jack Horner's shouted question was almost lost in the thunder of the plane's engine.

"Hell, we've got to!" Dusty bellowed back. "Keep low in your seat—and hold fast!"

As he spoke the last he slammed on opposite rudder, and banged the stick over. The cabin plane virtually groaned aloud in protest and it swished out of one spin and went whipping in again in the reverse direction. The sudden change caught the diving Black off guard for a second, and out the corner of his eye Dusty saw tracer smoke zipping past a dozen yards or so clear of the wings.

And then he saw it no more as the plane plunged into the enveloping mist of the cloud bank. A rasping sigh of relief spilled off his lips, but he still held the craft in its spin. Down through and out of the clouds he whirled. But the instant he was in clear air again he checked the spinning, pulled the nose up slightly and went power diving for some more clouds just below and about a quarter of a mile off to his right.

Though it was only a matter of seconds, it seemed years before his spinning prop churned into their fleecy whiteness. But, as he jerked quickly around in the seat, he glanced back just in time to see the pointed snout of the Dart cutting down out of the first cloud bank.

Whether the pilot spotted him fading from view, and hauled his speedy craft around in hot pursuit, Dusty didn't know. He was already in the clouds and he certainly, wasn't going to half-roll back into the clear to find out.

Hand rock-steady on the stick he eased the plane out of its dive and swung the nose up. A moment or two later he streaked up into the clear, cut sharply to the right and tore back into some more clouds. And for the next half hour he maintained a zig-zag cloud-to-cloud course until finally he was twenty-five thousand feet in the air and skimming across the crest of the topmost clouds.

Then and then only did he relax.

"Well, chalk up one for the poor people!" he grinned at Agent 10. "Bet that guy is biting his buttons off by now!"

The other didn't answer. A worried frown creasing his brows he stared moodily ahead. Dusty nudged him.

"Come up for air, kid!" he grunted. "The big bad mans is gone!"

Young Horner nodded absently, ground a balled fist into the palm of the other hand.

"Yeah," he mumbled. "And a damn neat bit of work, too, Dusty. But I don't feel so good."

Dusty stiffened, shot him an alarmed glance.

"Your wound? Is it—?"

"Hell, no!" the other cut in. "I don't know but what we'd better turn back!"

"Turn back?" snorted Dusty. "Back to Washington?"

"Yeah! The Dart got under my skin. When they come chasing you by air—and it's a cinch it's you they're after—way the hell down here, the answer must be mighty important."

"Check on that," said Dusty. "And it's all the more reason we should keep on high-balling to the general. He should be told about it, and told about it damn quick!"

"Yes, that's true," murmured the other grudgingly. "But he's on a secret mission—and these damn Blacks are perfect at adding two and two and getting the right answers. They must know that you're headed some place—on business."

Dusty didn't answer for the moment. He nosed down until the bottom half of the ship was plowing through the crest of the cloud.

"Sure they must know," he finally said. "But the point is, they don't know where! And in another half hour or so it will be dark enough for us to fly crow-line to T-Fourteen. Until then, we'll just float around up here, and not take any chances."

AT THAT moment the red signal light on the radio panel started blinking. Glancing at it, he hesitated, then reached out and snapped on contact, and spun the wave-length dial. He didn't get anything out of the cabin speaker unit until he'd reached a marking low down on the dial. But when it came through they both sat up straight and stared at each other. The cabin speaker unit poured out a long stream of staccato Black Invader jargon.

"What the hell? It's—!"

A savage gesture by Jack Horner cut short Dusty's outburst. The Intelligence man sat rigid, head slightly turned, eyes narrowed to slits. Clamping down on his curiosity, Dusty forced himself to wait for the other's next move. Two, three, four minutes dragged past and then the crazy gibberish coming from the cabin Speaker died off into silence.

"You get some of it, Jack?" he asked eagerly. "What was it about?"

The other gave him a queer look.

"You!" he said. "It was about you."

Dusty smothered the curse of impatience that came to his lips.

"Thanks!" he snapped. "Clear as mud! Somebody asking what I wanted for Christmas, I suppose? What the hell do you mean, it was about me?"

"I didn't get it all," replied Horner. "But enough. Black H.Q. has sent out a general order to all their stations, known and secret, to kill you at all cost. To kill you on sight!"

Dusty grinned, tightly.

"Still as popular as ever," he grunted. "That all they said?"

"No! Every Black agent was ordered to send in an immediate report on his activities."

Dusty gave him a keen glance.

"You mean to say they ordered that when they undoubtedly knew someone who knows their language might be listening in?" he asked. "Hell, Jack, that doesn't make sense!"

"On the contrary, it does," the other replied. "We've been expecting some move on their part for quite some time. They know that we know. As regards their agents—we don't know where they are. And their telling them to send in reports doesn't help us in finding out. The only possible thing we can expect is that this new move of theirs is about due. And if surprise isn't important—which it wouldn't seem to be—they should worry whether or not we know that something's due."

Dusty made no further comment. He nosed the ship down all the way into the clouds, bent forward and studied his electro-magnetic compass and course calculator. Then he put the nose dead-on for T-Fourteen.

As the minutes dragged by, the clouds through which they plunged grew darker and darker until, finally, when they shot out into clear air for a short space of time, night had fallen. Throttling a bit, Dusty let the plane slide down until he could see winking lights on the ground. There he leveled off, checked his exact position, and found that he was within twenty minutes of flying from T-Fourteen.

"Twenty minutes more, kid," he grunted at young Horner, who had long since lapsed into thoughtful silence. "Any particular spot we sit down on? I believe there's a small emergency field close to T-Fourteen—a couple of miles north. And how do you expect to get in touch with the general?"

"Know the street and number of the house," was the reply.

"Think you can get closer to the west side of the town than that emergency field?"

"Easy does it," Dusty told him. "Land in the main street if we have to. Keep your seat until the car stops!"

Throttling back to almost idling speed, he sent the plane floating down and to the right. Off to his left he could see a few winking lights on the ground, marking the location of Jackson. Using that as a guide he drifted lower until the outskirts of a completely darkened village loomed up ahead of him. And a few minutes later he had touched rubber and was gently wheel-braking to a full stop in a small field, less than a quarter of a mile away from the nearest house.

Cutting the ignition he nudged Jack Horner.

"End of the line!" he grunted. "All out! Now it's your turn to do the honors."

The Intelligence man climbed out of the ship without speaking. And as Dusty followed him, he saw his pal unholster his automatic and palm it in his right hand. He moved closer to him.

"We shoot on sight, kid?" he grunted. "Or what? Why the cannon?"

"Just in case," was the low reply. "Follow me. It isn't far."

Falling in step Dusty trailed his pal toward the nearest house. Agent 10 passed it without giving it a glance. But Dusty did, and he was surprised to see its apparent dilapidated condition. It was the same with the next house and the next, and the next. In fact, the narrow night-darkened street down which they walked rapidly was as a street of a forgotten village—a village

52

that had been completely deserted and left to the ravaging of time. A hundred questions came to the tip of Dusty's tongue, but he held them back and silently followed Agent 10's fast pace down the street.

AS THEY reached an intersection, young Horner turned sharp left, continued on for three or four blocks, and then turned sharp right. Two more blocks and then they swung sharp left again, but stopped dead in their tracks.

"Halt! Put up your hands!"

The sharp command cut the blurred darkness behind them. Dusty's hand inched toward his unflapped automatic, but he didn't touch it. Agent 10, in front of him, had raised both his hands high above his head. A split second later, as the Intelligence man turned slowly, one word came from his lips.

"Duluth!"

Hardly had it died to the echo than a flashlight beam sprang into life and "centered" them both in its rays. Dusty, who had also turned, blinked into the dazzling beam and sensed, rather than saw, two figures moving toward him.

"All right, gentlemen, at ease! Couldn't take chances, you know, even though we expected you."

The light moved up, outlining a smiling face for a second, then winked out. But not before Dusty had caught the glint of an oak leaf on each shoulder strap of an Intelligence staff uniform. Then he felt Agent 10 brush past him; heard his startled words.

"Expected us, major? How the devil did you know we were coming here? How'd you know who we were?"

A soft chuckle in the darkness.

"Afraid I can't tell you, Lieutenant Horner," said a voice. "You'll have to ask the general. Now, if you'll just follow us."

Dusty only moved because Jack Horner gave him a tug on the sleeve. Mind a muddled conglomeration of conflicting thoughts, he automatically followed the two blurred figures as they led the way down the street, turned into a narrow alleyway between two ramshackle buildings, and stopped at a door at the far end. A few knocks, the creak of the door swinging open, a few mumbled words, and the next thing Dusty realized he was in a low-ceilinged room, in the center of which glowed a single bulb.

He glanced at the two figures ahead. One was the smiling Intelligence major. And the other was a granite-faced staff sergeant, with a sub-machine gun cradled in his arms. The click of the door shutting caused Dusty to half turn. A staff corporal, also armed with a sub-machine gun, was standing guard at the door.

Frowning, Dusty shot a glance at Agent 10. The man was staring at the Intelligence major in baffled amazement. But there was no trace of alarm in his expression. Just baffled and befuddled wonder.

"This way, gentlemen."

The staff major was opening a door on the far side of the room and beckoning to them. Dusty moved forward with Jack Horner. The door led to a small corridor, at the end of which was a short flight of steps leading down to the cellar. They all stopped after they had entered a brilliantly lighted room that contained nothing but a few chairs and a table. The staff major motioned to the chairs.

"Be seated, please," he grinned. "I'll tell the general you are here."

Dusty sank into the nearest chair, and stared scowling at the major and the sergeant as they disappeared through a door leading off to the right. The instant it closed, he snapped his eyes around to Agent 10.

"What the hell, Jack?" he got out in a low voice. "You know them? Where the hell are we?"

The Intelligence man was scowling at the closed door, and slowly shaking his head from side to side.

"I don't get it," he mumbled. "Don't get it at all! Yeah, I know them both—the one upstairs, too. All from the department. And this is the place we were heading for originally. But, did you hear him? Hear him say we were expected? How could they possibly have found out?"

Dusty grunted, puffed his cheeks and spilled air out through pursed lips.

"I've been in lots of screwy places!" he murmured. "But this dump sure takes the chocolate-coated propeller! I don't think there's a soul living in any of those houses we passed."

"There isn't," Agent 10 replied. "The whole village was abandoned several months ago. An epidemic of infantile paralysis broke out. The authorities couldn't check it in time—so the whole village was condemned. The War Research Bureau has been using it since then. In secret, of course."

The rest he left unsaid. At that moment the side door opened, and the big, broad-shouldered figure of General Horner stepped into the room. As one man, Dusty and Agent 10 sprang to their feet and saluted smartly. The chief of Intelligence returned it with a short nod, fastened his steel-blue eyes on Dusty.

"Well, Ayres!" he boomed. "Still lucky, eh? It's a miracle how you came out alive from that motor crash! But what the devil are you two doing here?"

The last was directed at Agent 10. But Dusty blurted out the words before his pal could speak.

"How the hell did you know about my crash, sir?"

The general grinned.

"I saw you," he said bluntly. "Also saw that staff car chasing you, as you two tried to reach the field. Incidentally, we captured those rats, and they're where they won't do any more chasing cars for a long while!"

Dusty stared at the man as though he were seeing a ghost.

"You—you saw us?" he gulped.

"Exactly," nodded the general. "More of that, later, perhaps. Now, why the devil are you two here?"

Dusty and Agent 10 exchanged glances. Young Horner nodded.

"It's your story, Dusty," he said. "You'd better tell it."

For the second time, Dusty related every incident that had happened to him since he left the home drome of High Speed Group 7. As he talked, General Horner's face became grim, and his eyes narrowed under shaggy brows to sparkling slits. And when Dusty had finished he continued to hold the pose, not moving a muscle.

"Mlada! Mlada!" he suddenly breathed fiercely. "Damn! If Sixteen had only lived a little longer. Poor devil—and we thought he'd died, long ago. I wonder—I wonder!"

The tantalizing silence that followed the last was like salt in a raw wound to Dusty.

"Pardon, sir," he said. "You wonder what?"

The chief of Intelligence looked at him without actually seeing him. And when he talked, his voice seemed to come from far away.

"I wonder if you've stumbled upon the key to the whole blasted mess," he said. "You see, we know the Blacks are preparing a new offensive. Every indication points to it. There hasn't been a shot fired on the northern front for a week. Neither our Pacific nor Atlantic fleets have even sighted a rowboat! Apparently, only Black agents are doing anything. And the hundred or so we've captured, have sealed their lips. Even the firing squad doesn't budge them. They face it with smirking expressions, damn them!"

"And your agents, sir?" Dusty asked. "They've discovered nothing?"

GENERAL HORNER didn't reply for the moment. He swiveled his eyes around and allowed them to rest on his son's made-up figure. Presently he shook his head sadly.

"Nothing!" he grunted. "Absolutely nothing! Every available man has been put on the job—but no one has found out a thing."

"But an offensive of such proportions as you infer, sir," persisted Dusty, "can't be prepared overnight. Surely, your men in

Black territory must have spotted movements of troops and equipment and so forth!"

"They did!" the other snapped back. "But it doesn't mean anything. Simply various Black units exchanging positions in the line. Ordinary routine procedure."

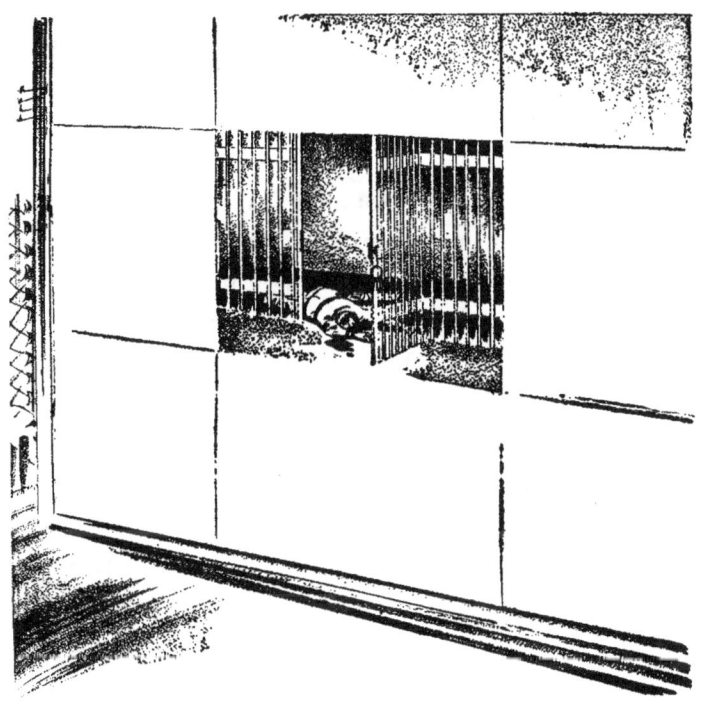

"And you still believe an offensive is due?" echoed Dusty.

"I know it!" the words were thundered out. "All that's taken place is simply a bluff for our benefit. It's the silence before the storm. And I wish to God I knew where the storm was going to break."

Heavy silence settled over the room for a moment or two. It was Agent 10 who finally broke it. He spoke to his father.

"There's no reason why it couldn't come from Europe, sir," he said quietly. "Our reports show that the Black forces holding the Canadian front are not over-equipped with supplies. And our Atlantic blockade hasn't exactly helped them. The destruction by Ayres of their receiving depot at Shoal Harbor, NF-Eight, three weeks ago, must have been a mighty big loss to them."

"Yes! And what?" the senior officer asked sharply.

"The fact that they are so anxious to get Ayres," young Horner replied. "Their strongest position, right now, is Europe—St. Albans, if a wild guess means anything. As we all agree, they believe that Sixteen told Ayres something. And it is my hunch that it was something to do with the coming offensive. If not, why the general broadcast to all Black agents to report?

"And why the general broadcast for Dusty's scalp? The answer is, that what Sixteen tried to, but didn't, tell Ayres hooks up with Black European operations against the United States! Otherwise, why should they become so alarmed, and go to such measures to get Dusty, if the knowledge locked in Sixteen's brain was to be confined to their operations in Europe alone? And last, why was poor old Sixteen kept alive for so long by Mlada? He's killed more than one of our agents."

"He's right, sir!" Dusty blurted out, as the other stopped. "Jack's right, I'm sure. We'll find the answer to all this in Europe—at St. Albans!"

The senior officer seemed unimpressed. Rather, he seemed grudgingly depressed.

"You may be right," he grunted. "But St. Albans is over four thousand miles from here. And this damned Mlada is a phantom. I've had agents after him ever since the beginning. And not one of them has even seen him—let alone spy on his activities. Even the few English agents that escaped capture have been unable to accomplish anything. The whole of England and Scotland and Wales is overrun with Blacks. A fortress that even a flea couldn't get into, to say nothing of getting out again alive with information we need."

Dusty spoke in a steady, quiet voice.

"I'd say that the situation necessitates a try, sir."

The general bent sharp eyes on him.

"I expected you to say that, Ayres," he rumbled. "I know you'd try anything. But contacting that devil, Mlada, at St. Albans is a hopeless undertaking before it's even started. If my men who have been there since the very beginning couldn't *get* through, it stands to reason that you'd have even less chance.

Dusty squared his jaw.

"Sixteen got out, sir," he said.

General Horner smiled, almost paternally.

"Yes, that's true, he did. But—"

The rest was left hanging in mid-air, as at that moment the side door slammed open and the Intelligence major came dashing into the room.

"General! General!" he gasped. "We recorded his cell block. He's escaped! The guard is on the floor—dead, I'm sure!"

The senior officer whirled on him.

"What?" he roared. "What the devil are you talking about? Who's escaped?"

The other fought desperately for breath.

"That Black prisoner you put in solitary!" he yelled. "The man

Captain Ayres captured. Ekar! The one who called himself the Avenger! He's gone—escaped!"

CHAPTER 5
DUSTY TAKES THE STICK

THE MAN'S shouted words were like bombshells exploding inside Dusty's brain.

Ekar! Hell, he'd forgotten about that rat. Sure he'd captured him! He and Curly and Biff had brought the rat back from NF-Eight after they'd smashed hell out of Shoal Harbor area.

Ekar—the fiend inventor of all the Black Invader chemical war weapons! Ekar—the devil who had wiped out Louisville Base, Cleveland Experimental depot, and Factory Four area with his last hell creation, radio-controlled chemical mist bombers.

Hardly realizing that he was moving, Dusty leaped forward and grabbed the major by the lapels of his tunic.

"Ekar escaped?" he thundered. "How the hell do you know? He was here? Here in this place?"

"No, hell no!" the other snapped, pushing him to one side and addressing the general. "It's still in focus, sir. You wished to—"

He didn't finish for the simple reason that the chief of Intelligence was bounding past him and through the door. Spinning, Dusty followed him down a short narrow corridor and through a door into a large room bathed in the subdued glow of fused mercury lights.

His first impression was that he had stepped into the control-room of a powerful broadcasting station. All four walls seemed lined with a million different electrical instruments. Then he suddenly noticed that the rear wall was a huge mirror of a sort of greenish-blue glass. In the center of the mirror was a second one, a tenth smaller in size and placed flat up against the larger mirror. A picture was pasted on the small mirror. It was the picture of a prison cell, obviously taken from the corridor outside.

The heavy barred door was half open. From the lock, suspended a ring of keys. On the floor inside was the huddled figure of an American soldier, lying face down. Blood from a jagged wound in the side of his neck stained the floor.

Close beside him was a tray, upside down, and a foot or so beyond, three broken dishes and a cup. The cup was unbroken, tilted up on its side, and running out from it a pool of dark liquid—unmistakably, coffee.

"Damn, damn! Have you got through to them yet, Barrows?"

General Horner's thundered words caused Dusty to notice the staff sergeant seated in front of a radio panel in the left corner. The man half turned; moved a phone back from his ear.

"Yes, sir! All patrols are out, now. He can't possibly get away!"

"The devil he won't!" boomed Horner. "Focus all cells, man—everyone in the city. Perhaps we can spot him. No, sit there at the set. I'll focus."

As he talked, the chief of Intelligence went over to a small panel fitted with two rows of single throw switches and rheostat dials. Using both hands he closed the switches and turned the rheostat knobs.

Dusty watched him in frowning silence. Then, suddenly, out of the corner of his eye, he caught flickering light from the double mirror. He turned toward them, and gasped aloud. The large mirror had become transformed into a squared pattern of pictures. Each picture was of some building, street, or street intersection in the national capitol—and they were all moving pictures!

Through dumbfounded eyes he saw people moving, cars passing by, a company of marching troops and a battery of artillery. It was like one great composite picture of Washington, thrown onto a screen in squared mosaic form. Hell, one of them was the tarmac of the Washington military field. He could even see his X-Diesel ship in the line of planes in front of the hangars.

Then, suddenly, movement in the picture on the center mirror caught his eye. It was then that he realized that his first impression had been wrong. It also was a moving picture—not a photograph stuck on the glass.

Two medical non-coms were laying out a stretcher in the corridor in front of the prisoner cell. They went inside, picked up the limp figure and put him on the stretcher. One of them threw a blanket over him, then each catching hold of end grips, they picked up the stretcher and moved out of the picture.

PERHAPS IT was a minute, perhaps five that Dusty stood rooted to the spot staring at the conglomeration of squared pictures of Washington. Even though it was night, in the glow of the street lights every detail showed up clearly.

It was as though he were standing in twenty different places throughout the Capitol at the same time. The spot, however, that interested him most was the damaged building front into which the Black agent had crashed the staff car. The car wreckage had been removed, and the gaping hole in the building hastily boarded up.

"So that's how he saw! Well, I'll be damned!"

The gasped, half choked words at his elbow caused Dusty to look around. Agent 10, his eyes out a mile, was standing beside him. He started to speak, but the booming voice of General Horner, who stood glaring at the composite picture, drowned him out.

"No use, I'm afraid! The devil's probably under cover somewhere. Barrows! Send orders through, under my code number, to search every blasted nook and cranny in the city. Watch all dromes, all roads, and all railroad stations. I want a net flung around the whole place. Yes, notify every unit! We've got to get him."

"Yes sir! At once, sir!"

Barrows turned back to his transmitter tube and started rattling code signals out over the air in a sharp, snappy tone. Chin sunk on chest, brows furrowed, and hands locked behind his back, General Horner fell to pacing restlessly up and down the length of the room.

He'd made about ten complete trips when Dusty suddenly stepped forward and took hold of his arm.

"I'd like to speak to you alone, sir," he said.

The senior officer stopped short, glared at him as though noticing him for the first time.

"Huh? What? What do you want?"

"To speak to you, alone sir," repeated Dusty. "No. To you and Jack."

The other's scowl deepened.

"What about?" he growled. "Can't you see I've got enough on my mind?"

Dusty didn't bat an eyelash.

"We all have, sir," he said evenly. "An idea just came to me—perhaps it will help."

General Horner hesitated, finally shrugged.

"God knows most anything will help now!" he boomed. Then turning to the Intelligence major, he snapped, "Keep them all in focus. And keep Barrows at it. If anything breaks, let me know at once. I'll be in your room upstairs!"

Without waiting for the other's salute, he nodded his head at Dusty and Agent 10 and stalked out of the room. Presently they were in a room on the next floor that contained an army cot, a couple of chairs, and a table spread with a miscellaneous collection of personal effects.

"Well, Ayres," the general turned on him. "What is it? Get it off your chest!"

Dusty scowled at the floor thoughtfully a moment, then raised his eyes to the other's face.

"That thing we've just been looking at, sir," he said. "Would you mind explaining it? Something like the Telerad screen, isn't it?"

General Horner's face clouded up, and his features twitched angrily.

"You've got me up here just to explain that confounded thing?" he thundered. "Dammit, don't you realize—?"

"Certainly!" Dusty rapped back at him. "As much as you do, I think! And if that machine does what I believe it does, it may be the one thing that will help us!"

Dusty's words snapping out like machine-gun bullets wiped some of the anger from General Horner's face. It was not the first time that the pilot had talked toe to toe with him, and in times gone past his words had meant plenty. The senior officer sucked in his breath, shook his head.

"No," he said. "It really has no connection with the Telerad development. It works on an entirely different principle. Invented by a man named Cook—call it the C-Ray. Briefly it works on the principle of photo-electric short wave cells that record light wave vibrations. So far, tests have proved it successful up to a distance of about two thousand miles.

"The single recorder—that center picture you saw—can be operated up to twenty-five hundred miles. The C-Ray recording cells look like, and are about the size of, an ordinary pocket flashlight. They can be placed anywhere. For tests we placed them at various spots in the capital. The lens—which is the secret of the whole thing—absorbs the light wave vibrations of whatever is in front of it just as the lens of the everyday camera does. At the receiving end there is another C-Ray cell in perfect light-wave synchronization with the recording cell. It, in turn, transfers those vibration-waves to a focusing plate which presents them to the eye in shadow form, or, in other words, the grays and the whites and the blacks of a definite picture. To a certain extent it is a form of television—the difference being that the C-Ray cell is less complicated, that it can record long range views, operates solely on the light wave principle, and is portable at any time to any place. The focusing equipment for the twenty-five hundred mile single cell can almost be fitted into a suitcase."

"Or even an airplane?" Dusty asked eagerly, as the other stopped.

"Why—yes! That's one thing Professor Cook has had in mind all along. To perfect a single cell set for airplane use. That center one you saw is his first completed unit."

"Then you mean, Dusty cut in again, "that the C-Ray doesn't require ground station current, or anything like that?"

General Horner snorted with impatience.

"I just told you that that single unit is adaptable to airplane use!" he growled. "The focusing equipment receives its power from what Cook calls the Compact Block. I understand that it's a multiple arrangement of dry cells in solid form hooked up in series to the new Stevenson midget generator. Well, that's the thing briefly. If Cook were here he could give you a more scientific explanation. Now what the devil's on your mind?"

"One more question, sir," Dusty said. "I take it, that the whole thing is a secret?"

"Naturally," the other snapped. "Outside of Cook, Major Hendricks, the sergeant, the corporal and myself, you two are the only others who know of the C-Ray. Excluding myself,

Cook and the other three haven't been away from this damn village in months.

"No one—I'm sure of it—no one else even dreams that they are here. Officially, they died in action six months ago. Since then, they've sacrificed everything to work with Cook.

"And, now, by God, success! We'll show those damn Blacks a thing or two now. With the aid of the C-Ray we'll know every damn move they make. Let them even get hold of one of the cells. It'll do them no good. Cook assures me that no one can discover the secret of the recording lens. He alone knows that. But, in case he dies, the formula process has been locked in the War Department vaults. If he dies, Cook has made it possible for us to still carry on with the manufacture of the recording lenses!"

General Horner suddenly stopped and shook himself like a big, shaggy-haired dog.

"But we're just wasting time!" he growled at Dusty. "Now, what the devil do you want to speak to me about?"

The pilot grinned, leaned forward.

"Thanks to Cook, sir," he said, "it'll be a cinch. We'll be able to find out an answer to this Mlada and St. Albans business in no time."

Horner gave him a piercing look.

"What?" he roared. "You mean—?"

"Sure, I do!" Dusty cut in. "A few of those C-Ray cells placed in the St. Albans area and we can just sit back and watch what goes on. Maybe, even get one in Mlada's H.Q. Too damn bad they don't record the voice, too."

The senior officer blistered the walls with an explosive curse.

"Are you mad, Ayres?" he roared. "Have you gone completely, stark crazy?"

Dusty kept his voice under control, even though wild excitement surged through him.

"Why no, sir," he said. "But such a thing would be a godsend, wouldn't it? We all believe that St. Albans holds the key to Agent Sixteen's words, don't we?"

"Yes, yes, of course we do!" the general snapped irritably. "But the C-Ray won't help us. In the first place it would be impossible to get any C-Ray cells into the area. And in the second place, the distance is too great to even hope that the receiving unit would focus anything."

"On the contrary, sir," Dusty said, "a plane flying well within the distance limit, and equipped with a focusing unit, would, get everything."

The senior officer snorted, gestured vigorously.

"Rubbish, Ayres!" he boomed. "You're shooting at the moon this time. Do you think that the Black blockade of the entire European coast and half of the Atlantic would close its eyes to an American plane? Why, you're crazy! But that's even putting the cart before the horse. You'd first have to get C-Ray cells in the St. Albans area. Are you thinking of doing it by thought transference? Why—why, it's ridiculous—absurd!"

Dusty went red to the ears, and his voice became keen-edged as he spoke.

"So you have said on a few other occasions, sir!" he got out. "And this is another emergency that requires emergency measures. If hell is brewing at St. Albans, and if it proves to be a gigantic new drive against us, the C-Ray and every other damn thing we've developed to fight the Blacks with, may never be of any use to us.

"I'm still thinking of Agent Sixteen. He sacrificed his life in an effort to warn us! Warn us about what? Something going on at St. Albans that we don't know about—and which the Blacks are scared stiff that we do! The C-Ray is our best bet in trying to find out. If we don't put it to the crucial test—and damn soon—we may find out what's happening after it has happened, and too late to do anything about it!"

Dusty's voice had gone up a dozen keys in fury tone, but he stopped abruptly as the Intelligence chief put up a restraining hand.

"Take it easy, Ayres. Perhaps I was a little too blunt in my remarks. But look at it from the sane point of view. How could you, or any one else, accomplish the thing you suggest? The distance is too great. And I repeat—I doubt if even a flea could get close enough to St. Albans, let alone an American plane. You'd be killed before you'd even sighted the islands."

"That way, I would, yes," Dusty replied. "But here's my plan— shoot holes in it, if you wish. I'll take off in a Black cabin plane—one of those folding-wing submarine jobs that we've captured. Like that one that's now on exhibit in Washington. O.K.?

"I'll meet one of our patrol X subs, say, fifteen hundred miles out at sea. They'll take me abroad, and run the Black blockade as close into the English coast as possible. Then, under the cover of darkness they can launch me and slip back to sea.

"I know the St. Albans area well. Learned it when we were doing courtesy maneuvers with the British air force five or six years ago. Anyway, I can buzz over the area and drop a few of those C-Ray cells by small chutes. One of them, at least, is bound to light in a good spot.

"Then I can simply buzz around, fly deep into Europe if necessary, and watch what's going on. By arrangement beforehand the X sub will always be at a certain spot at certain times. Thus I can always get back for fuel, and report to the commander what I see for resignaling back to Navy H.Q. and you.

"In that way, I won't have to risk operating the plane's set and perhaps be picked up by their radio-broadcast detector units. Hell, perhaps the whole thing is a risk! But, don't you see, sir, it's one we've got to take!"

The chief of Intelligence sat scowling dubiously, and before he could speak, young Horner leaned forward.

"I'd like to get a word in, if I may," he said. Then, at a nod from the senior officer, he turned to Dusty, "I agree with you, but only in part. True, it's a risk we've got to take. But it isn't a risk for just one man alone. Now—wait a minute! I think I know the St. Albans area even better than you do. Dropping the C-Ray cells by chute is just the same as popping marbles down a dark well. You say that at least one of them would light on a good spot. Maybe, and maybe not. Perhaps there are several good spots there—and I imagine there are. But we've got to be sure—absolutely sure that we get them where they'll do the most good. That will be my job! I'll—"

"Hey! Wait, kid, you—"

"Shut up!" Agent 10 snapped. "I think your plan of getting to the St. Albans area is perfect. As the general knows, we have got our agents into Europe. Getting them out again with news was where we met with failure. But with the C-Ray, that part is automatically eliminated.

"The news will come out, regardless. So you do the flying and the contacting with the submarine, and I'll put the C-Ray cells where they'll do the most good. Hell, it won't be the first time that I've dropped in on those bums by night chute. It will almost be like going back home."

Agent 10 turned toward his father.

"In fact, sir, I may be able to contact our men who are there now and possibly reorganize the system a bit for better results in the future."

Dusty took hold of his arm, squeezed hard.

"Nothing doing, Jack," he said firmly. "You're in no shape to tackle that kind of a job. Tell you what—Curly will do the flying, and I'll drop in on them. And, just in case, Biff can tag with Curly to help him on the flying, or even work the rear gun if they get into a jam. Nix! There's plenty for you to do right here in this country!"

His pal seared him with a single look.

"Don't be a sap Dusty! It's a job for all of us, and you know it! I'm in condition to tackle anything. Even if I weren't it wouldn't make any difference in this case!"

Ignoring Dusty, young Horner turned back to his father.

"We've got to try it, sir," he said evenly. "As I said, I agree with Ayres—it's a risk we cannot afford not to take!"

THE SENIOR officer continued to scowl dubiously. But little by little an expression of reluctant resignation seeped into his moon-shaped face. Presently he let go a long sigh.

"Yes, I suppose you two are right," he murmured. "Damn Ekar, I had been hoping to break him down and get him to talk. Maybe he could have told us something."

"We got him once and we'll get him again, sir," Dusty broke in hastily. "Now about this Black cabin job. They have one at the Baltimore naval base. How long would it take Cook to fit it with a C-Ray cell focusing unit? Tonight? By the way, where is he?"

General Horner nodded to the right, toward a closed door.

"In there asleep," he said. "Poor devil has been up for five days and nights Tuning. Hate to wake him, even now. But—yes, he can get it fixed by a bit after midnight, I guess. We've a plane here. The corporal's a pilot. But, dammit, if I only felt sure that you'd get through all right."

"Don't worry, we will, sir!" Dusty exclaimed. Then, addressing them both, "I'm on my way to get Curly and Biff. We'll meet you at the Baltimore base at midnight, sharp. In the meantime, arrange with Navy H.Q. for one of our patrol subs to pick us up, say, just before dawn. I'll leave that to you, Jack. By the way, better have them stand a double guard at Baltimore. Don't want to let the whole world in on it, you know."

Agent 10 nodded.

"Right," he said. "But watch your own step, Dusty. You know that Black order we heard. Why not stick here—leave Curly and Biff out of it this time? Maybe that would be safer."

"Maybe," said Dusty. "But with four of us, there's just that many more chances we have of making the grade. Besides, those two bums would never forgive me when I got back."

"I hope to God you do get back!" General Horner sighed heavily. "If only there were some other way—"

"There isn't," Dusty said. Then Baltimore at midnight! See you later!"

With a grin and a parting salute for them both, Dusty turned and walked out of the room.

CHAPTER 6
BIFF CRASHES THROUGH

FIVE MINUTES later he was retracing his way through the deserted village back toward the small cabin plane. He hadn't wanted to leave so soon. There was still plenty of time, and he would have liked to inspect the C-Ray focusing unit in detail and to have had a talk with Professor Cook. But he couldn't take time for the simple reason that he feared that General Horner might change his mind and throw out the whole crazy plan. Yeah, it was a crazy plan. No doubt of it. But, hell, other crazy plans had worked out O.K. in the end. So this one had to, too! Or else—

Ekar escaped.

As the thought came back to him, he gritted his teeth, balled his fists.

"Horner should have slapped him up against the firing wall, and let him have it!" he grated to himself. "Six feet under is the only safe place for that breed. Hell, hope I meet up with him again after we get through this job."

Suddenly Dusty stopped dead in his tracks. He was about a hundred yards from his ship; could just barely see its blurred shape. But it wasn't the ship that pulled him up short. Rather it was the faint, almost indistinct, throb of an airplane engine high overhead.

Experience having tuned his ears to the slightest warning sound, he knew at once that the powerplant aloft was not American-built. The throbbing note was decidedly different. In short, a Black Invader plane was patrolling the night-darkened heavens. Half turning, he frowned back in the direction from whence he had come. Everything was blurred in darkness, and shrouded in complete silence. There was not a sound, save the faint throb of an engine high overhead. Was it by accident that a Black night raider was over this particular spot? It sounded as though the pilot was loafing about in a series of lazy circles. No, no he wasn't. The sound was fading off to the west. The plane was going away.

Breaking into a run, Dusty pounded ground the rest of the way to the cabin ship. Skidding to a halt by the cabin door, he strained his ears for the sound of the mysterious plane. But it had apparently gone away for good.

"Got his nerve with him!" he grunted, climbing into the ship.

"Buzzing way the hell down here! Huh, wonder if it's that same Dart, that tried to pick on us?"

Shrugging the unanswerable question aside, he booted the electric starter, caught the engine on the first rev, and sent the ship tearing across the field.

The instant he cleared, he banked around and flew due south, following the course of the Mississippi for a good seventy-five miles. And all the time he maintained constant vigil above and behind for a possible glimpse of tell-tale exhaust flames. Once he thought he spotted a tiny flicker in the dark sky, but it disappeared instantly and didn't reappear again.

Finally, satisfied that he was alone in the darkness, he swung around, climbed up to twenty thousand and set a compass course for the home drome of High Speed Group 7.

One hour, two hours of uneventful, monotonous flying drifted into history, find finally he eased back the throttle and allowed the ship to go sliding down through banked clouds toward the field that was now well within gliding distance.

At fourteen thousand he cut out of the lowest clouds, and was able to see the faint twinkling of lights on the ground.

Relaxing the tension of his body, he started to steepen his dive when suddenly off to his right, and about five hundred feet above, the dark skies spat twin streams of jetting flame and a hundred trip-hammers rattled against his engine cowling. A split second later the glass cowling literally blew up in front of his face, and showered him with a million stinging barbs of slivered glass.

Caught cold, he staked all on slamming through a flash

double roll that virtually caused the wings to groan aloud in protest. But the unseen trip-hammers still smacked against the sides of his ship, and he even felt one of them tug at the left shoulder strap of his tunic.

THEN, SUDDENLY, a dozen or more searchlight beams below sprang into life and slashed the dark heavens with their brilliant shafts. It blinded him for an instant, but he instinctively whipped the ship into a savage spin and whirled down as certain death continued to smack and crackle about his ears.

A thousand feet lower, he hauled the plane out, and jerked up the nose. In that instant, he saw a shadow, sleek and black, tearing down. It spat fire and instinctively he steeled his body and jabbed his own trigger trips forward.

But only a short burst of five slugs or so ripped out of his guns before he cut his fire and bellowed in amazement. A second shadow was slicing down through the searchlight beams. Slicing straight down at the first shadow and raking it unmercifully from prop to tail wheel with hot, smoking steel.

The lower shadow, which took on the shape and lines of a Black Dart as a searchlight beam "centered" it, suddenly went skidding off to the left, rolled half over and went down like a stone. A moment later a great tongue of flame belched upward from where it struck the ground.

Dusty only gave it a glance, whipped his eyes back toward the second shadow. As it swung around toward him, and cut through a searchlight beam he saw the clean, perfect lines of an X-Diesel ship.

With a whoop he snapped out his hand to the wave-length

dial, spun it, and finished the whoop in a grating curse. The marksmanship of his mysterious attacker had been perfect as far as the radio panel was concerned. The set was in splintered shambles.

Unable to contact the X ship, and unable to see the personal markings on the fuselage, he slammed his own plane into a dive once more and went racing for the drome below.

A couple of minutes later he was taxiing up to the hangar line. As he legged out two figures came running up to him. One was Curly Brooks, and the other was Major Drake.

Curry grabbed him.

"You?" he shouted. "My God—what the hell? Where have you been? We've been going nuts!"

Dusty didn't answer. Another ship had landed on the field as he was coming into the line. It was an X-Diesel, and the pilot who climbed out of it when it stopped, was Biff Bolton. Dusty pounded over to him.

"Thanks Biff!" he exclaimed. "That's another one I owe you."

The big pilot stared at him in amazement.

"Gosh, was that you?" he exclaimed. "Thought you were a goner for sure. Gee! What—?"

He didn't have time to finish the question. Curly and Drake had plowed over. They both spoke in the same breath.

"What the hell have you been doing?"

Dusty raised a silencing hand.

"Hold it!" he snapped. Then to the C.O., "Let's get together in your office, sir. We've all got a lot to say, I guess."

The major simply nodded, turned and led the way over to the group office. Once they were all inside he faced Dusty again.

"Right, spill it!" he grunted. "You've given us all gray hairs! What the devil is happening?"

Dusty shrugged.

"Getting popular again with the Blacks, I guess," he said. "But, before I have my little say, I want to thank you again, Biff. That one was tight, and no fooling."

"Forget it," rumbled the big pilot. "We've been hearing that lug overhead all evening long. Been taking turns trying to find him. I was just lucky enough to be up there when you came along."

Dusty pursed his lips, nodded his head slowly.

"Should have thought of that," he murmured. "Naturally, they'd cover this drome, just in case I did come here. The bum probably picked me up in his night glasses."

"For God's sake, Dusty!" exploded Curly. "Will you please tell us where in hell you've been?"

"O.K.," the other shut him up. "Here's the whole story, as far as I know it."

And then in as few words as possible he told them everything, right from the beginning up to the present moment.

"This last mixup proves that they do want me bad, because of what they're afraid this Agent Sixteen told me," he finished. "That ship I heard over T-Fourteen—maybe an accident, maybe not. But whether yes or no, we've got to slide down to Baltimore Base without a single soul knowing it—not even the lads at this field, major."

"That can be done easily enough," the C.O. grunted. "You won't even have to take off from this field. Carter had a forced landing in the photo ship late this afternoon. Came down in that field back—: the old Merrick Knitting Mills. Throttle broke. He borrowed a car and came back. I decided to wait 'til morning before sending the greaseballs out. It's a simple job, though. Any one of you could fix it."

"Perfect!" exclaimed Dusty. "We take a car, as though we were going into town for a feed, but cut off on the Hartford Road. Sure, it's perfect, major!"

"That part of it, yes," nodded the other. "But I think you're mad, Ayres. I feel much the same as General Horner does—it'll take a miracle to get away with it. I'm afraid you don't truly realize what you're up against. I've heard of this Mlada, myself. He's an absolute fiend.

"And he's one rat I want to meet!" Dusty finished savagely. "Dammit, we at least owe it a try for Agent Sixteen's sake. He cashed in, trying. And we can't let him down now."

"Damn right we can't!" echoed Curly Brooks.

"Check!" rumbled Biff Bolton. "Always wanted a ride in a sub, anyway."

The last was so totally out of place and unexpected that the other three burst out laughing in spite of themselves. Major Drake finally sighed and gestured with both hands.

"I suppose there's no use in my trying to stop you," he said. "You'd go anyway. Damned if I don't think I'll change my name and enlist all over again. Then maybe I'll see a little action now and then. But—oh well, a million in luck, as usual! I'll be biting my nails until you all get back again. And—and somehow I feel that you will. Crazy fools, and drunkards—the Lord watches over both!"

"You can count on us to be back sir," Dusty grinned. Then to his two pals, "O.K., mugs, we'd better get going. You two get the car around in front of my hutment. Bring a throttle for the ship. I'm going to get into some different duds. Too many places in these for the breezes to get through. Be set in ten minutes."

WITHOUT WAITING, for them he ducked out of the office and ran over toward his hutment. The field was in darkness now, save for a couple of shielded hangar lights. The searchlights had gone out of action, but off to the west was a faint dull red glow marking the spot where the Dart had crashed and burned up.

Dusty paused outside his hutment door, stared narrow-eyed toward the red glow. For a moment it impressed him as being a sort of danger signal. Red—danger ahead! He smothered a curse, shouldered into his hutment and started pulling off his tattered clothes.

Going over to his locker, he pulled out an old uniform, and climbed into it. He was just hooking on his Sam Browne when a car siren blared outside the door, and Curly's voice came drifting through.

"Hey, snap it up, you! We can't wait for that steak!"

Dusty grinned, slipped his automatic into its holster, took a quick glance about the room to make sure he hadn't forgotten anything he might need, and stiffened, frowning. There was a sheet of paper pinned to the folded blankets on his bunk. And there was some writing on the paper. He reached the bunk in one leap, bent over the paper. There was but one short sentence. It read:

"Whom Ekar seeks, Ekar kills!"

Just that signal sentence, unsigned. Brows knitted, Dusty stared down at it silently, then cursed.

"He couldn't possibly have put that there!" he grunted. "So that means one of his rats is around—right here in Group Seven. Huh! Better tell Drake before I pull out."

Ripping the paper free he stuffed it in his pocket, bounded over to the door and dived through. As his feet touched the ground he tripped, grabbed frantically at thin air and went sprawling. In almost the same instant a rifle cracked and a bullet smacked into the door jamb, where a split second ago he had been standing. Again the rifle cracked, from the darkness off to the right. This time the bullet clanked against the right mudguard of the car.

"Hey! Dusty! What the devil?"

Curly cut off his bellow of alarm as Dusty practically threw himself into the rear seat of the car.

"Get going! Fast, Curly!"

The third crack of the rifle was partly drowned out as the car's engine roared up. Tires screamed as Curly swung the car around in practically its own length and went speeding away. Once out on the open road he eased up the speed a bit, half turned in his seat. Biff Bolton, beside him, also turned.

"Who was it, Dusty?"

"One of Ekar's boy friends, I guess!" Dusty shouted back. "Found a note on my bunk. Thank God I fell over my feet. With that light behind me I was a perfect target. Let her out for all she's got!"

Curly increased the speed immediately.

"A note?" he echoed. "From Ekar? How in hell could he—"

"Me too!" Dusty drowned him out. "So it couldn't have been. One of his rats, probably—just in case I was as lucky as I have been. If there were time I'd go back and smoke him out. But there isn't, so Drake and the boys will have to do it. Say, this all the speed in this tub?"

Curly's reply was lost as he fed the thirty-two small-bore cylinders under the cowled hood every ounce of hop they could take, and the car leaped over the headlight-flooded strip of roadway rushing toward it.

Two miles further on, Curly swung into a side road on two wheels, straightened out, tore across the Merrick bridge over the Connecticut River, and thundered through the small textile manufacturing town in a cloud of swirling dust. A mile beyond it, he careened the car up over a sloping embankment, plowed across a stretch of open field, and finally came to a halt close to a cabin photo plane on the far side.

"Douse the lights!" cried Dusty leaping out. "No need of asking for customers. Biff! Got that throttle?"

The big pilot was already thrusting the lever into his hand.

"Got a pocket flash, too, skipper," he grunted, as they ran over to the plane. "I'll hold it for you."

Climbing in through the cabin door, Dusty took the handy

wrench from the tool kit under the seat and went to work taking off the old broken throttle. Though he worked fast, it was almost half an hour before the replacement throttle was completely adjusted. But a minute after that he had the engine revving over, and was wheel-braking around toward the long end of the field. Another thirty seconds and they were in the air, climbing as fast as the prop could claw them up.

Taking no chances of being spotted from the ground, Dusty held the nose up until the altimeter needle quivered at the thirty-five thousand foot mark. Then he leveled off, settled back in the seat, and glanced at his watch. The hands showed exactly twenty-seven minutes after ten.

"Make it easy!" he grunted aloud. "Get there ahead of time, if anything."

"All right, kid, let's hear the rest!"

Dusty jerked around and stared at Curly.

"The rest of what?" he asked. "What do you mean?"

Curly leaned forward, grinned.

"The part you left out," he said. "The sub idea is a stall, isn't it? What's the real plan of operation?"

Dusty cursed.

"Of course the sub idea isn't a stall!" he shouted. "I told you everything I know. What's the matter, don't you want to—"

"Ixnay on that line!" Curly choked him off. "I mean, have we got to travel by sub? Why not, let's drive right over in the crate? We'd save all kinds of time, you know. Make it in seven hours easy—even in one of their pontoon jobs!"

"Way ahead of you, sweetheart!" Dusty replied. "Thought of

that, myself. But it's out! Too much chance of running into Black patrols that might get curious. And besides, we don't know how long we may have to stick around over there. Those

Blacks are funny, you know—they don't like to give fuel to the enemy!"

Curly made a noise in his throat.

"My error!" he grunted, relaxing back in the seat. "That's so, too. Sorry. But keep me in, coach! I'll fight!"

As the last remark was lost to the echo, silence settled over the cabin. Snapping on the instrument cowl light every now

Curly
BROOKS

and then, to check his course, Dusty held the ship on even keel, and let it slice through the night skies toward the Baltimore naval base.

In an attempt to kill time he mulled over the strange sequence of events which had befallen him since late afternoon. Each he mentally studied in detail, turning it this way and that in his mind in an effort to find something that in the rush and excitement he had missed or overlooked.

But the events as memory presented them were cockeyed enough in themselves, and he discovered nothing new. He finally finished up with thoughts of Ekar, the self-styled avenger of the Black Hawk.

KNOWLEDGE THAT that rat was loose bothered him more than the task before him. Having fought the man, and knowing full well of his merciless cunning, he did not entertain a single hope that General Horner's man-made net flung about Washington would trap him in its web.

So—where was the devil headed? Back to Black territory up north? Or was he planning to remain within the gates of the U.S. and re-strike at its vitals from within?

Hell, if it weren't for the St. Albans job, perhaps he could do something to lure the tramp out into the open, whet his hate and force him to show his hand. Yeah! Nothing would be more satisfying than to fill the rat's hide with hot slugs this time.

"Uh-uh! Now, what?"

Dusty heard Biff Bolton's exclamation the same instant that he saw the red signal light on the radio panel spring into life. He risked the cowl light long enough to glance at the incoming broadcast wave-length dial. The needle was at the S.O.S. Emergency reading. Shooting out his free hand, he snapped on contact and spun the dial knob to the tuning-in reading. The cabin speaker unit started crackling out sound, instantly.

"… stand by! All stations stand by. A warning! Enemy static-jam curtain established along entire Atlantic seaboard! Coastal patrol units are ordered to keep strict lookout for possible off-shore maneuvers by enemy ships or aircraft. Relay half hourly reports to H.Q. via Ten D-C Four. S.O.S. Emergency signing off!"

The speaker unit clicked silent and the red light winked out.

"So what?" growled Curly heavily.

"So maybe we'll do it your way after all," replied Dusty. "Don't know yet."

"Don't know what, yet?" Brooks snapped.

"Whether Navy H.Q. got through to the X sub we're supposed to meet," Dusty grunted back over his shoulder. "If they set up that static-jam curtain before Navy H.Q. tried to contact the sub—well we're in for a lot of flying tonight. However, we'll soon know. Hang on! I'm going down. Baltimore Naval Base next stop!"

CHAPTER 7
EAGLES EAST

AS DUSTY spoke he slid the throttle back, shoved the stick forward, and sent the ship slicing down out of the black sky. Twenty-thousand feet lower he found out, with an inward glow of satisfaction, that he had hit his objective right square on the nose. Off to his left were the lights of the city of Baltimore. And below him, on the southern side of the mouth of the Patapsco River, the Naval Base with its combination ground and water drome.

Spiraling down he waited until a bank of floodlights sprang into life, then straightened out and glided in to a perfect landing fifty yards from the hangar nearest the long concrete ramps that sloped down into the water. As he started to taxi closer however, he suddenly braked to a halt. A mechanic, waving his arms, was rushing out toward the plane. When he reached it, the man jerked open the cabin door and stuck his head inside.

"The fourth hangar up, Dusty!" came the familiar voice of Agent 10. "Go right in, and stick in the ship until I tell you. Be there almost at the same time!"

"Hey! Wait!"

Dusty let the rest trail off. Agent 10 had slapped the cabin door shut and was running up the tarmac toward the fourth hangar, three other figures in greaseball clothes trailing him.

"That was Jack, wasn't it, Dusty?" Curly asked. "Why the fourth hangar, I wonder?"

"Me too!" grunted Dusty, goosing the engine. "So we'll find out."

He wheelbraked around parallel with the hangar line and taxied toward number four. The three men in greaseball clothes were rolling open the wide doors, but they didn't snap on any of the lights inside the hangar. At a waving motion from the figure Dusty knew to be Jack Horner, he taxied the photo plane through the open doors and into the shadowy interior. The instant he killed his engine the doors were rolled shut and everything became pitch dark.

Footsteps sounded across the concrete, and the tiny beam of a pocket flashlight sprang into being.

"All right, fellows," came the low voice of Agent 10. "Climb out and follow me."

Holding back the countless questions on the tip of his tongue, Dusty obeyed. With his two pals at his heels he followed the flashlight beam directed on the floor, across the hangar and into a small replacement-parts room in back. There Agent 10 stopped and placed the flashlight on the edge of a bench so that its beam bounced off the opposite wall and filled the small room with faint light.

It was then Dusty realized that the three mechanics were also in the room. He turned to Jack Horner, started to speak, but the other cut him off with a gesture.

"Change with these lads, you fellows," he said. "Snap it up!"

"Huh?" Biff Bolton's deep voice echoed. "Change what?"

"Your uniforms!" young Horner clipped at him. "Got to make sure of this thing. Don't worry, these are department men. Hurry it up!"

Less than two minutes later, three pilots had become three greaseballs. And three greaseballs had become three pilots. Then Jack Horner addressed the newly created pilots.

"All right men," he said. "You know your act. Get going, and make it good!"

The three Intelligence men nodded and silently left the room.

When the sound of their heels clicking on the concrete floor of the hangar died away, Dusty took hold of Agent 10's arm.

"Why all that, Jack?" he asked. "Something gone wrong?"

"Not that I know of," replied the other. "But I just don't believe in taking chances. No telling who saw you lads land, so I arranged for this change over. The boys are going to hang around outside, so that any prying eyes can get a good look at them. And, we, the greaseballs, are going to saunter on our way. Get the idea?"

Dusty grinned.

"Leave it to you to plug up the holes, kid," he said. "You're dead right. Now, where's the ship? It's all set?"

"Yes. Waiting at the inner basin a mile south of here. We can take off whenever you're ready."

"Which is right now!" exclaimed Dusty eagerly. "But wait! Hold it! Here's something!"

In a few jerky sentences he told of the S.O.S. Emergency message. Agent 10 nodded.

"Yes," he replied. "We picked it up, too. But the static-jam curtain hasn't anything to do with us. Navy H.Q. contacted the X-Twelve sub over two hours ago. It's meeting us at five dawn, at AT-Seventeen. That's fifteen hundred due east of Ambrose Channel Lightship! No radio signals. They're using two green and a long red flash, at intervals of five minutes, commencing at four-thirty.

"The lights will be on the port bow, and the sub will be traveling five knots due east. No return signals from us. Their detectors will pick us up. We land a quarter of a mile from it, and wait for the sub to come alongside. O.K.?"

"Perfect!" breathed Dusty. "Let's get going. Fifteen hundred off Ambrose means a good seventeen hundred from here. So we've no time to lose."

"Right," Agent 10 nodded. "Now trail with me. Forget you're officers. Act like greaseballs. But I guess that won't be difficult. Come on."

DUSTY AND Agent 10 leading the way, Curly and Biff tagging behind, the four walked out a side door of the hangar and went shuffling down the tarmac toward the seaplane ramps. There they turned right, skirted the various drome buildings, and presently were making their way along a narrow dirt road that followed the shoreline south.

They had gone but a quarter of the distance when Jack Horner suddenly broke into song.

"Join me, gang!" he snapped under his breath between the first verse and the chorus. "A little harmony goes good with greaseballs you know."

The other three got the idea at once, and the night air was instantly blasted by Curly's high tenor, Biff Bolton's booming bass, and Dusty and Jack Horner somewhere in between. They passed a few groups of soldiers and received Bronx cheers. But they let the cheers go unanswered and continued nonchalantly on their way.

Eventually, though, a rifle bolt clicked and a sharp voice rang out.

"Halt!" Who goes there?"

Dusty cut off in the middle of a note, stiffened. But to his amazement, Agent 10 continued right on walking forward.

"Four greasemonkeys, sweetheart!" he called out. "Where's the damn tub we have to take back? Officers should take lessons in handling them things before they go out alone, huh?"

A guard in Yank uniform loomed out in the gloom.

"You guys, huh?" he growled. "About time you got here. This was to be my night off. Its right here. Watch your step. And how's for a ride back?"

"Okey, buddy!" Agent 10 replied cheerfully. "Come, gang. All aboard for a ferryboat ride."

As he talked, young Horner turned and beckoned to the other three. Silently they followed him down a sloping bank to the water's edge where a long motorboat was moored. The guard climbed in first and took a seat in the bow cockpit at the wheel. Dusty, Biff and Curly seated themselves in the middle, and Agent 10 took his place in the stern.

"Let her go, buddy!" he called out. "All lines aboard!"

Electric starting gears whined, the exhaust bellowed sound, and the boat shot out over dark water. Leaning forward on his seat, Dusty strained his eyes at the surrounding darkness. By the movement of shore lights he realized that the boat was swinging straight out into the bay. He wanted to turn and pop questions at Jack Horner, but he didn't. He simply sat still and told himself that Agent 10 knew what he was doing. All this was just another attempt to fog up any prying eyes.

Ten, fifteen minutes dragged past, and then the boat's engine went silent, the speed slackened and the craft slid quietly around in a wide half circle.

"Heads down!"

The command from the guard at the wheel was scarcely more than a low whisper, but it carried back, clear as a bell to those aft. Instinctively, Dusty ducked his head, at the same instant conscious of a dark shadow sweeping past a few feet above him. He twisted over, looked up and saw the faint outline of an airplane wing silhouetted against the carpet of dim stars high overhead.

"All right, fellows! Off the bow onto the pontoon. Cast off the buoy line, buddy, once we're on. Then make all the noise you can with that corn-popper!"

More whispered words. This time from young Horner's lips. The motorboat was alongside the nose of the pontoon. In quick, catlike movements Dusty stepped onto it, worked his way back to the pontoon strut step, and up in through the cabin door.

A well-shielded cowl lamp shed just enough light for him to see the pilot's seat. He slid into it, and waited for the other three to climb in. Agent 10, who was last inside, took the seat at his side and leaned toward him.

"Clear water ahead, Dusty," he said. "He's going to run that boat full out to make as much noise as he can. It should cover up our take-off noise considerably. O.K., start when he starts!"

The last had hardly left the Intelligence man's lips when the pounding roar of the motorboat engine blasted the silence. The instant the sound smacked against his ear-drums, Dusty thumped down on the electric starter, caught the engine on the first rev, and eased the throttle wide open. Less than thirty seconds later he had pulled the ship clear and was cutting up into black sky. At his side, young Horner chuckled contentedly.

"If that didn't work!" he grunted. "Then I'll give up!"

"Neat, all right!" Dusty replied. "He was another department man I suppose? Seems to me there were a lot of lads in on this."

Agent 10 shrugged.

"Had to be that way," he said. "We'd have been asking for it to just walk out and take this thing way from the base. So I arranged it this way. However, they don't know where we're headed. Or even what's in this ship. Cook and I installed the thing alone. No, wait a minute, kid. Let's not risk lights for awhile. Plenty of time for you to look at it. All very simple, as a matter of fact."

Dusty, who was reaching out his free hand to turn the shield of the cowl lamp so that clear light would flood the center panel on the instrument board, let his hand drop back, and grunted.

"Hope you're right, Jack," he said. "I rather expected to have a talk with Cook before we took off."

"Wasn't necessary," was the short reply. "Cook explained it all to me. Not much to it, as I said. Besides, it was dangerous for Cook to hang around too long."

Dusty stiffened, gave his pal a keen glance.

"Dangerous?" he echoed. "What do you mean?"

Jack Horner was silent for a long time. He only spoke when Dusty nudged him impatiently.

"I'm not sure," he said slowly, "but I think we were followed from T-Fourteen. I could almost swear that I saw the exhaust flash of a ship a couple of times."

The words sounded a note of eerie warning inside Dusty. He cursed softly, gripped the stick hard with both hands.

"Hell!" he snapped. "Why didn't you tell me before? Maybe we are—"

"No," Agent 10 cut him off. "I wasn't sure, absolutely sure, that we were followed. But, in case, I had the corporal take Cook off again and head south while I stayed behind. If we were tagged—that'll throw them off."

"Here's hoping!" muttered Dusty absently. "Possibly it was another of the bums looking for me. But I take it your dad didn't come along, eh?"

"No. He stayed back with the major to continue experiments with the squared plate. And thank goodness he did, too!"

"Meaning what?" asked Dusty.

"After you left," Agent 10 replied, "he had a change of heart. I had to do a lot of fast talking to stop him from calling off the whole thing. And if he'd been along—seen the exhaust flashes, too, that would have tipped the apple cart. He's banking, more than you realize, on Cook's C-Ray development. Incidentally, I made them both promise—had to."

"Yeah? What?"

At Dusty's question, young Horner reached forward, touched the C-Ray cell focusing plate panel on the instrument board.

"A promise that we would not let this fall into Black hands," he said grimly. "We're to take no chances—destroy it at the slightest sign of danger."

"But I thought the lens of the recording cell was the big secret?" said Dusty.

"It is," Agent 10 agreed. "A million of the recording cells wouldn't do them any good. But according to Cook, if they got hold of the focusing unit too, it is just possible they might discover the secret of the lens formula. Anyway, our orders are not to take any chances."

DUSTY MADE no further comment. Still holding the nose up, he relaxed in the seat and stared at the shadow-covered instrument board. He could just barely see the C-Ray focusing panel in the center, yet, clear enough for him to surmise its operation. To the left of the panel was a two-inch wide vertical strip of metal, and fastened to it six sets of small throw switches and rheostat knobs.

From in back of the strip, braided wires ran down to clipped-on terminals that studded the top of an eighteen-inch square box clamped to the floor of the cabin. From these terminals more braided wires ran up to the lower ends of six black glass tubes that extended an inch or so below the bottom rim of the focusing panel. What was behind the panel, he could not see.

Eventually, tired of looking at them, he bent forward and squinted at the altimeter dial. The needle was just short of the forty-seven thousand foot mark. Automatically, he leveled off the ship, but kept it on a dead-on course for AT-Seventeen. Then he relaxed in the seat again.

For a Long time no one spoke, the only sound being the faint throb of the engine in the nose drifting back through the sealed cowling. Below, above, ahead, behind and on both sides darkness blotted out everything.

Cloud layers had blanketed out the carpet of faintly twinkling stars and utter pitch darkness seemed to close in on Dusty and virtually press against his body. Repeatedly he shifted his position in the seat, or bent forward to look at the electro-magnetic compass directional finder. The action wasn't that he was afraid he might be getting off the course. He knew perfectly well that he could blind-fly to AT-Fourteen and smack it right on the nose. Rather, it was something to do—something to ease an eerie tensing of his body every time he gave himself up to absent thought.

The devil of it was the feeling was not new. He'd experienced it countless times before. It had always come to him as a form of advance personal warning of impending danger. In relaxed moments he had often tried to analyze it—determine definite reasons for its existence. But always be was forced to simply credit it as the so-called sixth sense, and let it go at that.

The main thing, though, was that the familiar feeling was taking hold of him again. Did it mean anything this time? Or was it simply because of the tensed monotony of the flight; because of the period of time which must elapse before anything definite would happen?

He cursed inwardly, swallowed hard and turned in the seat.

"Why so silent, children?" he grunted back in the darkness at Biff and Curly. "Don't tell me you're asleep!"

"No," came back Curly's voice. "Just thinking. How about a

little planning while we have the time? After we get aboard this damn underwater tug, then what?"

"As I told you," Dusty replied. "The sub takes us in as close as it can. Then when everything's clear, we'll be launched. You two will drop Jack and me as close to the St. Albans area as possible. And—"

"No, Dusty!" young Horner broke in savagely. "Hell, man, you can't go over the side! Me, I've got a Black uniform under this, and my make-up kit. You'd be spotted before you got a hundred yards. No, I'm counting on you three to do the flying, and to get word back of whatever the C-Ray cells I place about show you."

"And just leave you there, eh?" snapped Dusty. "Like hell!"

"But you poor boob!" yelled young Horner. "That's my job. I've been there before. That's the sort of thing I'm trained to do."

"Not when you're a week out of the hospital!" Dusty rapped back. "Now—hold your horses! We'll argue that out after we get aboard the X-Twelve. Besides, I've got a better plan—one that you'll even agree to. Haven't worked out the details yet. Tell you about it later."

He stopped short. The red signal light on the radio panel was blinking.

"So!" he ejaculated. "We're clear of the static-jam curtain, anyway!"

Reaching out, he fumbled for the contact switch, snapped it on, found the wave-length dial and turned it. A quarter of a turn around the dial and the cabin speaker unit crackled sound.

It was sharp staccato sound. Dusty instantly recognized it as Black Invader high speed dot-dash signals. He turned to Agent 10, who had leaned forward and was listening intently. Dusty sensed, rather than saw his pal stiffen and grip the sides of his seat with both hands. And he could almost feel Biff and Curly straining forward in their seats.

One, two, three minutes clicked past and then the dot-dashing sounds subsided, and faded out entirely.

"Yeah?" Dusty breathed, when Agent 10 didn't speak. "What now?"

Young Horner cursed softly before he answered.

"What the hell? What the devil could they mean by that?"

"By what?" Dusty snapped impatiently.

"That was in Black Navy code to their Atlantic fleet commander," replied young Horner, more to himself. "I didn't get it all—they've changed the code a bit. But he said, "Objective accomplished. Will proceed with program. Stand by for further orders! Damn him! Where the devil can he be? And what in hell does he mean?"

A sharp tremor, like an electric shock, whipped through Dusty as he shouted the question.

"Who? Who are you talking about?"

"The man who signed that message," Agent 10 replied heavily. "It was signed—Ekar!"

CHAPTER 8
HELL'S SUBMARINE

F OR A full thirty seconds after young Horner spoke, there wasn't a sound in the interior of the cabin. A rumbling curse from Biff Bolton's throat finally shattered it.

"Ekar! That bum again, eh? Then the tramp musta made good on his getaway!"

The sound of the voice jerked Dusty out of a seething trance. He bent forward, pushed up the cowl lamp so that its rays flooded the entire instrument board. But he turned it down almost immediately and groaned.

"Damn, should have done it in the first place. Hell!"

"Done what?" came Curly's sharp question.

"Taken a squint at the station directional finder," replied Dusty bitterly. "Could have found out where it was coming from. The needle's at zero now. He's gone off the air."

"Listen!" exclaimed Agent 10, excitedly. "Contact Washington H.Q. See if they're still maintaining that static-jam curtain."

"By God, yes!" echoed Dusty. "I get you! If the curtain's still there, it means that Ekar is this side of it, and heading for Europe—St. Albans! That's the reason, that's the reason! It must be. They static-jammed the coast so that warning couldn't be sent to our ships on patrol. Sure as you're a foot high, that's the reason."

In quick movements he snapped on transmission contact, and spun the dial to Washington H.Q. reading. But he didn't speak into the transmitter tube. He didn't have to. The high-keyed whine that poured out of the cabin speaker unit gave him the answer. The entire Atlantic seaboard of the United States was still static-jammed.

"Ekar, headed for Europe!" he breathed fiercely, snapping off contact. "By God, we must be on the trail of something big. Damn, I feel it! If something wasn't due, that rat would have headed for Canada. Come on, get moving! We've got things to do!"

The last was directed at the plane, and he emphasized his words by banging the throttle wide open. A glance at his watch told him that there was still an hour and a half of flying between their present position and AT-Twelve far ahead in the darkness.

Ninety minutes, each of which seemed an eternity in itself before it slid by into forgotten history. Eventually the darkness became fused by the first faint line of coming dawn low down on the eastern horizon, a crack of light that became bigger and bigger, changing the heavens to a shadowy blurred gray.

A hundred times Dusty checked his course, and a hundred times found that he was not even the fraction of a degree off the true setting. His eyes ached and smarted from constant vigilance ahead. But he hardly noticed it. His whole body was as taut as a bow-string. With tantalizing slowness, the hands of his watch crept past four o'clock, reached four-ten, then four-fifteen.

Suddenly Curly's sharp voice smacked against his ears!

"Down there—to the right! Light flashes!"

Dusty's eyes leaped in that direction. Nothing but murky shadows at first. Then he saw it—two quick blinks of green light, followed almost instantly by a long red flash. They were so faint that at first he believed his eyes were playing him tricks. For the last hour he had been visioning those flash signals in his mind. But Biff Bolton's rumbling voice confirmed Curly's discovery.

"Yup! That's it all right. Must be a low fog under us blotting out the signals!"

Eyes glued to the spot, Dusty let the plane drift forward at half throttle. And then, presently, he saw them again. There was no mistake about it this time—two quick green and a long red. Automatically he glanced at his wrist watch. The time was exactly twenty-three minutes after four.

"Must have picked up our engine and started the signals ahead of time," he grunted to himself.

He switched his eyes to the compass directional dial, stared at it a moment, and frowned. Without turning his head he spoke to Agent 10, pointing at the dial.

"What do you make of that?" he asked. "I figure that we're still a little over a hundred miles from the middle of AT-Fourteen. The sub must have run east to meet us."

He stopped, jerked up straight. From out of the murky shadows far ahead came a muffled, resonant booming sound. Just for a fleeting instant he heard it, then it was lost in the throbbing beat of the plane's engine.

"You fellows hear that?" he asked quickly.

"Yes!" they answered in tensed chorus.

Then Curly continued.

"Sounded like an explosion!" he said. "Something blowing up, way the hell ahead."

It added nothing to Dusty's thoughts. Something had blown up all right. A terrific explosion far out of sight—there hadn't even been the faintest flicker of light in the distance. He stared down and off to the right, sucked in his breath sharply. The signal flashes were no longer coming at five-minute intervals. They were being repeated over and over again, one right after the other. Unconsciously he tapped rudder, swung the plane that way, and sent it sliding down.

"Something's doing ahead," he grunted. "That's why they came east to meet us. Guess they heard it, too. Want us to get down quick. Jack! Take those marine glasses there in the box. I'm going lower, but I just want to make sure. See if you can get a look at it."

He didn't bother to turn as he spoke. But movement at his side told him that Jack Horner was doing as he asked. Eyes fixed on the blinking signals below, he held the ship in a glide seaward, waiting breathlessly for Agent 10 to speak. The altimeter needle was at the three-thousand foot mark, and the plane was still sliding down through murky shadows, all the more deepened by a low fog, before Jack Horner cried out.

"It's her all right! I can just see the X-12 on the conning tower. She's headed east. The forward hatches are open, and the pick-up boom is swung out. Yup—it's the X-12!"

A pent-up sigh of relief slid off Dusty's lips, and was echoed by grunts from Biff and Curly behind him. Easing the throttle all the way back, he flattened the glide considerably and pointed for a spot about a quarter of a mile off the port bow of the underwater craft.

AT TWO thousand feet the fog thinned, and at one thousand it faded away entirely, leaving nothing but faintly fused murky light over the water. A desire to look to the right swept over Dusty, but he grimly held his eyes on the murkiness ahead. It was going to take every bit of his flying skill to sit down without snubbing the pontoon nose in the rolling waves. Time enough to look toward the submarine later.

Pulling up the nose until the craft was but a couple of points or so on the safe side of stalling speed, he virtually "felt" his way down the last hundred feet. Those in the cabin with him realized the ticklishness of the job, and hardly a man of them even so much as took a deep breath.

Mushing, floating down through ever changing shadows. And then, suddenly, there was sluggish rolling movement directly under the pontoon; deep, heavy shadows that seemed to rise up toward the ship, slush down and fade away. Steeling himself, Dusty pulled the stick all the way back into his stomach.

"Hold everything, gang!" he snapped between clenched teeth.

For the fraction of a second the plane seemed to hang motionless in mid-air, then it sank with a sickening sensation. There was *a swish-clump*, like a man striking the flat of his hand against the side of an empty keg.

The plane tipped over to the left, quivered, then swung up and over to the left. Then it righted itself again, and mushed forward, faint white spray, like ghostly shrouds, spewing up against the windows of the cabin.

"Boy! You sure earned your wings that time!"

The words came from Curly like air being spilled out of fire-billows. Dusty swallowed hard, breathed an inward prayer of thankfulness.

"Sure won't make a habit of it!" he muttered. "And that's a cinch! Now, providing they don't ram us, we'll all be having a good stiff one soon. And it'll help, too!"

As he spoke he unsnapped and lowered the spray-drenched side window and peered out. Cold, salt-tanged air blew against his cheeks. He sucked it into his lungs and felt fifty per cent better. And at just about that moment a muffled hail came to him from across the dark waters.

"Put on starboard wing light! We're coming up on that side. Stand by to fold wings when ordered!"

"Biff! Curly!" snapped Dusty as he turned on the right wing light. "You two be ready to crank the wings back. I've got to keep us headed into the wind. Steady, everyone!"

WORKING THE throttle and pontoon rudder Dusty kept the seaplane mushing slowly into the wind at practically no speed at all.

Presently, out the corner of his eye, he saw a knife-edged, pointed shape come into view. Like a ghost it sidled closer and closer to the plane. Then in the faint glow of light that came up through the opened hatchway, he saw the long sleek forward deck of a submarine.

Figures in fatigue clothes were running along the deck. Three of them, braced against the chain rail, caught hold of the right wingtip and fended it off before it slammed into the upraised

108

"FOLD WINGS AND STOP ENGINE" CAME THE MUFFLED ORDER

hatch cover. One of them boosted himself up on the wing. Dusty could hear him making his way along to the roof of the cabin were the hoisting rings were fitted.

A moment later there came the wheezing of a compressed-air winch on the submarine, and a clanking sound as the man on the top of the cabin worked the grappling hooks into the hoisting rings. And then, the muffled order, "Fold wings and stop engine!"

Snapping off ignition, Dusty waited while Biff and Curly knocked out the front spar locking bolts and then turned the master wheel that controlled the wing-folding ratchet gears. A minute later a faint jar running through the plane told them that the trailing edges had contacted the stop-pegs aft, and that the wing was folded back.

At almost the same instant came the command from above. "Stand by to hoist! Hoist away!"

With the hissing of escaping compressed air, the plane trembled from prop to tail, rose straight upward, and swayed gently like the pendulum of a huge clock. Leaning over toward the open window, Dusty stared down.

The plane was hanging suspended above the open hatchway. Down in the compartment below was the padded cradle for the pontoon. Blurred figures stood waiting. On top-side other figures were pushing against the pontoon, guiding the craft around so that it could be lowered.

A moment later, more hissing of compressed air and the plane sank down through the open hatchway, and settled with a gentle bump on the pontoon cradle. A command from the man atop the cabin was followed by the clanking of loosened grappling hooks and then the heavier sound of the hatch covers dropping into place.

Dusty turned to Agent 10, grinned at him in the dim light.

"And so far, so good! Who's the skipper of this sub? He rates plenty of praise—couldn't have done the job neater."

"You're right!" nodded young Horner reaching toward the door. "Lieutenant Commander Standard, I believe. Let's go to his quarters now. He doesn't know what he's to do yet. And I bet he's wondering plenty. What the hell—we're already under way!"

A throbbing motion was proof positive of that fact. Pushing Agent 10 ahead of him, Dusty climbed out through the door, ducked under the folded back wing, and jumped down off the cradled pontoon. He turned and flung out a helping hand to Biff and Curly as they piled down after him. Giving them a grin he turned and followed Agent 10 who was making his way clear of the tail of the plane.

But as they ducked under the elevators and stepped out into the clear, they all stopped dead. In fact, they froze stiff in their tracks. Ten feet in front of them stood four sailors in fatigue clothes. The fatigue clothes didn't mean a thing. Each sailor held a revolver, and all four muzzles were trained on them.

For a split second Dusty's thoughts were knocked haywire. He unconsciously jerked his head around as he heard sounds behind him. There, ten feet away also, were four more sailors, each one covering them with a revolver. Then came Agent 10's enraged outburst.

"What the devil's the meaning of this? Where's Commander Standard?"

One of the sailors spoke.

"Coming! But don't move, or we'll shoot. Put up your hands, all of you!"

"Listen, you fathead!" roared Dusty, swaying forward. "Don't you realize that we're—?"

Crack!

The revolver spat flame and sound. A bullet ripped through the slack of Dusty's left sleeve and *whanged* against armor-plating in back of him. In spite of himself, he jerked his head around expecting to see one of the other four sailors stretched out on the steel deck. But they had moved to the right, and were not within a dozen feet of where the bullet had zipped past.

"Put up your hands! I'll come closer next time!"

Dusty turned back, slowly raised his hands, and held his rage in check as one of the sailors searched him from head to foot and relieved him of his automatic he had strapped about his waist under his mechanic's clothes. Then the man did likewise to Biff, Curly and Jack Horner. Stepping back he took up his position with the other three.

Cold, clammy fingers clutching at his heart, Dusty stared at them—blurted out the words in a bitter voice.

"You—you're not Yank gobs!"

The original speaker of the four said nothing. He simply smiled—a twisted, crooked smile that made blurred red film over Dusty's eyes. Had he not suddenly sensed movement to his left he would undoubtedly have hurled himself forward in

112

spite of those steady guns. But he didn't. Caught himself in the nick of time; looking to the left.

A bulkhead door was swinging open, and a figure in a make-shift Black Invader uniform was stepping through. The side of the face nearest Dusty was hidden by bandage that circled over the head and under the jaw. Then the figure turned face front, started to walk forward but stopped dead. Cruel, deep-sunken eyes opened wide with dumbfounded amazement, and the jaw sagged down as far as the bandages would permit.

But the facial expressions of the figure were lost on Dusty. It was the face itself that suddenly sent his heart pounding savagely against his ribs. The face, even with its bandage was etched in fire upon the mirror of memory.

It was the face of Ekar, the Avenger!

CHAPTER 9
ACTION, C.O.D.

FOR ALMOST a full minute not a sound, save the pulsating throb of Diesel engines, broke the silence that literally crushed itself down upon the room. Everyone held the tableau like statues of chiseled marble.

And then, suddenly, roaring laughter burst from Ekar's throat.

"You! You!" he bellowed, striding forward. "I did not even think—did not even suspect! You, and you, and you, and you! *He-e-e la-a-a zo!* The god of war has indeed blessed me with good fortune this night!"

Shouting the weird Black Invader cry of salutation, the man

jabbed a pointed finger at each of them. Quivering with berserk rage, it was all Dusty could do to hold himself in check. But he did—did for the simple reason that way down deep inside a tiny still voice sounded a note of warning.

The thought-blasting amazement at Ekar's entrance had been mutual. He had not expected to see them any more than they had expected to see him. Until that part of the mystery was cleared up, there was not much to be done. Not much to be done? Hell, what was there to be done?

To blot out his own soul-searing thoughts, Dusty grinned as Ekar finally turned back and confronted him.

"So you didn't expect us, eh?" he said. "Well, that's one more for our side—and a few additions on the way!"

The Black's eyes narrowed, and he seemingly made no effort to keep the puzzled expression from his face.

"No," he said. "I did not expect you. We expected the plane, with four aboard. But you four, no!"

The man paused long enough to chuckle. Dusty grabbed at the straw, turned to Curly who stood next to him.

"Thank God, kid!" he exclaimed. "This means the other fellows made it!"

Curly's face was blank for just the fraction of a second. Then he took the hint and nodded vigorously.

"Yup! They must have made it!"

"Made the X-Twelve?" Ekar barked. "I think not. The X-Twelve is now at the bottom of the Atlantic. We destroyed it not half an hour ago."

"You destroyed it?" demanded Dusty.

The other shook his head.

"A figure of speech, that 'we', captain," he said. "We on this craft had nothing to do with it. Other ships took care of that. Our task was to greet you four. No, not exactly you four! *He-e-e la-a-a zo!* It is like a dream come true. I rather expected you to be dead, captain. As I once remarked, you do, indeed, lead a charmed life. Rather, had led a charmed life, I should say."

Dusty shrugged, calmly lowered his upraised hands.

"Oh, I get around," he said casually. "But the surprise is mutual. I'm curious, though. Did a vision come to you, or did a little bird tell you about this plane? I don't recall that we put an announcement of it in the papers."

Ekar smiled, bowed slightly.

"Would that you were a Black Invader, captain," he said. "Much as you have troubled us, I cannot help but admire your cool courage. One would almost think you didn't believe there was such a thing as death. This plane, you ask? We found out about it, as we find out all things regarding your country's movement.

"Two minutes after your navy department sent instructions to the submarine X-12, we knew about it; knew of the point of contact, the time, the signals to be used, the type of plane, and the fact that four persons would be in it."

The Black stopped short, snapped his eyes toward Jack Horner, and curled his lips back in a scornful grimace.

"That's what secret agents are for!" he said. Then with a harsh laugh, "Ours have been trained over a period of years—long before we delivered the first blow. Yes, our agents are trained to accomplish things!

"And, incidentally, they are not amateurs in the matter of disguise, either. You, Lieutenant Horner, I recognized the instant I set eyes on you a few minutes ago. You believed me to be in that paper prison of yours, eh? Bah! I could have done on any other day what I did today. But it served my purpose to permit my enemies to help me recuperate."

As Ekar finished the last, he threw back his head and roared with laughter. Then the laughter faded out and his eyes slithered back to Dusty's face again.

"Yes!" he snapped. "To recuperate from injuries suffered at your hands, captain! You understand, of course, I shall repay you tenfold!"

"Make it an even dozen!" Dusty clipped at him. Then as a sudden thought came to him, "Of course you were on your way to find me! Running like hell away from America? Maybe you figured on finding me at—St. Albans, eh?"

Ekar's eyes flew open wide, and a sharp exclamation in his native tongue rushed off his lips. His eyes literally burned into Dusty's face.

"So?" he spat out. "So?"

"So—what?" grunted Dusty, inwardly tingling with the realization that his blind shot in the dark had struck something.

"So you do know something?" the other murmured, almost absently. "They told me that perhaps you knew—that you must die at all costs. I thought it best not to linger and enjoy that little spectacle. Besides, they were waiting for me elsewhere.

My friends had risked too much in helping me escape, for me to ignore them. But—you do know, eh?"

AS THE Black talked, his eyes had wandered toward the forward end of the compartment. Hardly realizing that he was doing so, Dusty half turned his head, followed the man's gaze. What he saw answered a question that had been in the back of his mind ever since the moment he had collected his thoughts after the surprise of seeing Ekar. How the devil had the man got this far out to sea?

He saw the answer now, forward and in front of the pontoon cabin ship. A small, low wing, two place amphibian of the type used by both sides for coastal patrolling. This one was a Black Invader ship. Perhaps it had been kept hidden somewhere along the two thousand-odd miles of American eastern coastline. Or perhaps it was part of the submarine's equipment and it had been flown in to pick Ekar up at some desolate pre-arranged meeting place.

"Yes, I know all about it," lied Dusty as he felt the other's eyes upon him once more. "But I'm not the only one, sweetheart. The big surprise is yet to come! The big surprise for you! Tough, too—after pulling such a neat trick.

"You must have worked fast, removing your real number and painting X-Twelve on the conning tower in its place. And I suppose that static-jam curtain your boy friends hung up on our eastern coast was just an additional precaution, eh? Just in case we tried to check with those ashore?"

"Not you, captain," smiled the other. It wasn't entirely for your benefit. There was the possibility that the real X-Twelve might see our ships closing in on it, and perhaps warn your naval headquarters. *We* couldn't afford to take that chance.

"We wanted to find out just why one of our captured planes, with four Americans aboard, wanted to meet a submarine. Fortunately, this craft happened to be in the vicinity when the original instructions were radioed. That put us in the ideal position to do the finding out, as you might term it. And, by the way—"

Ekar turned and addressed the remainder at Agent 10.

"You might tell Washington Navy H.Q. that it's time for them to change their code again. That is, unless they insist upon telling us everything! But there—I'm afraid that you won't be able to tell them. They'll just have to find out for themselves!"

Young Horner said nothing but the look that flickered across his face told Dusty that their thoughts were the same.

The one weak link in the entire plan bad been that which they hadn't even given a thought to—confident that it was the strongest. That was Navy H.Q. contacting the submarine X-12. Hell! The whole first part of the plan had been sent out over the air in a secret code that wasn't secret at all!

Inwardly Dusty kicked himself. Kicked himself for not giving more consideration to Curly's suggestion. Damn, if they'd only taken a chance and slammed right on across without bothering about the X-12!

"And now that we've cleared up a few minor points for each other, captain," Ekar's pleasant voice broke in on Dusty's bitter train of thought, "perhaps you'll be kind enough to explain one of your first remarks. I believe you said, "This means that the other fellows made it! What other fellows? And just what was their objective?"

Dusty almost permitted the blank expression to come into his face and give him away. But he remembered making the remark, just in time. He grinned at the Black, reveled inwardly with realization that Ekar was more than a little worried. The man's every movement fairly shouted that fact. Why? He didn't know. But that didn't matter. Ekar was worried about something—plenty worried, too!

"Oh, you mean the carrier squadron?" Dusty stalled. "Well, you'll find out about that soon enough. Incidentally, this tug has been underway since we came aboard—not heading toward the French coast are you?"

The Black started violently, whipped his hand to the side, and snatched a revolver from the hand of one of the men in sailor fatigue clothes. Eyes holding Dusty with the very intensity of their glare, he jabbed the revolver muzzle against the Yank's chest.

"French coast?" he practically hissed. "What's at the French coast? Tell me—tell me at once, or I pull this trigger!"

Dusty's stomach did loops, and he could feel cold drops of sweat trickling down the small of his back. But he didn't flinch the fraction of an inch.

"Pull it, then!" he grated between clenched teeth. "I'd rather pass out from a steel slug than go up in small pieces from a bomb. That right, fellows?"

"Damn right!" came back Biff, Dusty and Jack in chorus.

"You lie! It's a bluff! I see now, you know nothing!"

Ekar had stepped back a pace. Dusty expelled the air from his lungs.

"Thanks," he said. "You were damn near caving in my left ribs. But you're right—I don't know a thing. Just an old lie builder-upper that's me. Now whose turn is it next?"

The Black ignored him. He turned to the nearest sailor, rapped out something in his own tongue. Then giving the man the revolver, he turned and went striding out through the door by which he had entered.

"Steady! Or I'll pull the trigger!"

DUSTY CHECKED his unconscious movement in the direction Ekar had taken, turned around to look right down the muzzle of a revolver. Its owner had it trained on a spot right between his eyes. Dusty shrugged.

"I believe you would at that," he said quietly. "They ought to make you an admiral for having so much good sense. Pulling that trigger would save your boss an awful lot of trouble. And I'd be able to keep my secret, then!"

The Black sailor frowned and stared at Dusty in silence. A blind man could see that the Black was thinking rapidly—turning over Dusty's words in his mind. The Yank flashed him a final grin and calmly turned to his pals.

"Put your hands down, fellows," he said quietly. "If they shoot, that'll be their tough luck. Get what I mean? Guess it's curtains for us, anyway. But what the hell—we didn't figure that both ships would get through. One of us was bound to miss."

Curly Brooks' lips curled back, and a defiant look came into his eyes. He started to speak but Dusty beat him to it.

"Cut the sob stuff, Curly!" he said sharply. "And don't be dumb. We've lost, and that's all there is to it. It's up to the other lads, now. See?"

As he spoke he looked directly into Curly's eyes. The lean pilot frowned faintly, looked just a bit puzzled. But though he missed the play, Jack Horner didn't. He laughed bitterly.

"You're right, Dusty," he said. "Can't say I want to die, but—the other lads must have made it. So I guess we can't kick. Cheer up, Biff! Hell, didn't the ten of us draw lots? We all had an equal chance to get in on the aircraft carrier plan, you know. It was just our tough luck that we drew the X-Twelve."

Biff Bolton, closed one eye, fixed the other on the Black sailor nearest him.

"Yeah," he rumbled hazily. "Sure. But, I've got a mind to pop one of these mugs, just for the hell of it."

"That would just be asking for it sooner, Biff," Dusty told him. "Can't you see that this lad here is just itching to pull the trigger? And he'll do it soon enough. We're not of any use to them now. Just extra cargo. Ten to one—when Ekar comes back, he'll give the order to shoot. He's a busy man, you know. Can't afford to waste time on us. We've told him all we know."

Though Dusty's words were directed at the big pilot he kept looking at Curly all the time. Suddenly the frown faded from Brooks' face, and a light of perfect understanding came into his eyes. Dusty sighed inwardly. Curly had caught on to the stall game at last. The lean pilot's next words proved it.

"Five-fifteen!" he exclaimed, glancing at his wrist watch. "Hot dog! It can't miss now!"

"Silence! All of you!"

The Black, whom Ekar had spoken to, snarled out the words. In turn he glared at each and made menacing gestures with his revolver. And then he turned to the next sailor, rapped out something, and started for the side door. Before he reached it, though, it opened and Ekar reentered the room.

The sailor immediately clicked his heels, and started talking to Ekar in low hurried tones. Dusty watching the Black ace saw his good eye narrow and the frowning lines come into his forehead. The Yank's heart pounded against his ribs in joyful exultation. He didn't have to understand Black Invader jargon to know what the sailor was talking about. One guess was enough.

The man was repeating their conversation to his superior. And Ekar was becoming more worried than ever. As the sailor finished, he slithered his eyes over toward the prisoners, let them come to rest on Dusty. A moment later he pushed the sailor to one side, walked forward.

THREE FEET from Dusty he stopped and stood staring hard at the Yank pilot. Though Dusty kept a half smile on his lips, inwardly he was teeming with suppressed excitement. The dropping of the fake hint about the French coast and airplane carriers was getting the desired results.

Ekar and the others were not sure of the next step—particularly, if it was to shoot the four of them down. The cold hatred in the Black's eyes fixed on him was proof positive to Dusty of what the man wanted to do. But sane reasoning was holding Ekar in check.

He had not expected to capture these four prisoners. The element of surprise had thrown him momentarily out of stride, and the seeming hopeless resignation of his prisoners to their immediate fate gave him cause for much serious thought. In short, his own eyes betrayed the troubled thoughts behind them.

Dusty widened his grin.

"Aren't you going to pull that trigger?" he grunted. "I was just telling the boys that you would as soon as you got back."

"You seem rather anxious to die, captain," the other said in a flat voice. "Perhaps it pleases me more to let you live—for a little while!"

Dusty shrugged.

"The longer we all stick here, the better it'll suit me," he said. "There are others to take care of Mlada without our help."

"Mlada!" Ekar fairly shouted the word. "What do you know about Mlada?"

Dusty didn't answer at once. The mention of the name Mlada, had created an electrified tension in the room. Ekar, and the others, had stiffened automatically and were now peering at him through narrowed lids.

But it was not their appearance that sent a little tremor rippling up and down Dusty's spine. It was the flash glimpse that he caught of Jack Horner out the corner of his eye. The Intelligence man let his eyes flicker from Dusty to the sailor nearest him, back to Dusty again. Then, he gave a quick short nod of his head.

A signal? Perhaps. Dusty had to chance it anyway. He couldn't expect to keep these Blacks guessing all night. The time had come to play the last card in the game—to stake everything on one last throw of fortune's dice.

"What do I know about Mlada?" he echoed at Ekar. "Quite a bit. To begin with, his little St. Albans secret is going to be knocked into a cocked hat. I was told this morning that—"

He didn't finish it. Ekar, eyes wide, had unconsciously swayed toward him. All of the Blacks as a matter of fact, were virtually hanging on his words. And in that split second of time, Dusty hurled himself into action with every ounce of his strength. With the speed of a striking cobra his left arm shot out, hooked around Ekar's neck and jerked the Black up against him.

In the same instant Dusty flipped out his right and snatched the revolver dangling from the fingers of the nearest Black sailor. A twist of his wrist and he had the butt in his palm and his finger crooked about the trigger. Without uttering a sound he pulled the trigger and smashed a hunk of steel right through the forehead of the second sailor.

"Drop your guns—drop them!"

His words were like the echo of the single revolver shot.

"Right—drop them!"

Agent 10's words whipped out right after Dusty's. Out the corner of his eye, Dusty saw his pal. Young Horner had moved with him—done almost the same thing. He'd spun on the nearest sailor, torn his gun free and was now holding the man clamped against his as a shield against the remaining Blacks. And with the gun he covered the three sailors who had been standing in back of Biff Bolton and Curly Brooks.

Ekar, locked tight against Dusty, struggled to get free and

started to cry out something. But Dusty simply crooked his arm tighter against the man's throat and words simply became gurgling sound.

Three seconds at the most, and then five revolvers clanked down onto the steel deck, and five pairs of arms shot upward. And then Biff and Curly flew into action. In less than no time they each scooped up a gun and joined Dusty and Jack Horner in covering the others.

"Biff!" Dusty snapped, twisting away from Ekar's clawing fingers. "That coil of line over there on the left. Get it and truss up these guys. If they object—let 'em have it!"

Big as he was, Biff Bolton moved like greased lightning, and in a matter of two minutes, no more, seven Black Invader sailors were trussed hand and foot, and flat on their backs on the deck. Three of them were "sleeping" as the result of Biff's gun contacting their foreheads.

That accomplished, Dusty twisted his body and shoved. Like a plane leaving a catapult, Ekar shot across the room, slammed up against the steel plates, crumpled and went down in a silent heap.

"Never mind him, Biff," said Dusty, as the big pilot started trussing up the man. "I've got uses for him."

"Don't mind me, kid," mumbled Curly, rubbing a hand across his forehead. "I'll wake up eventually. But what the hell is the plan now? God, am I tipping my hat to you and Jack!"

Dusty caught Horner's eyes, grinned.

"The old team work, eh?"

"Yeah," the other nodded. "I could see that you were working up to it. But—well, what now?"

Dusty pointed at Ekar.

"Climb into his clothes—bandages, too," he said.

"Huh?" ejaculated young Horner. "Listen, we've got to get the hell out of here, fast!"

"Sure," nodded Dusty. "That's my idea. But, do you think that the other bums on this tub are going to sit back while we hoist the plane out?"

Agent 10's face went grave.

"That's so, too," he grunted, casting his eyes upward toward the closed hatches. "What do you plan to do then?"

"The only thing we can do." Dusty replied quietly. "Take complete charge of the damn tub!"

CHAPTER 10
ESCAPE!

"TAKE COMPLETE charge? Are you nuts? There's at least sixty men on this boat!"

Jack Horner's words poured off his lips like water going over a broken damn. Dusty raised a silencing hand.

"Steady, kid," he cut in. "Figure it out. As things stand now we're just so many fellows in a trap. To get away we've got to do two things—stop the sub, and get the plane out into the water. That can only be done from the control-room.

"Now if I know subs, well find the commander and his executive officer in the control-room. All orders go out from there.

Now for a couple of Yanks to try and reach the control-room, would simply be asking for a slug in the back. But Ekar herding me up there, would be different. So you become Ekar. The bandage will help plenty.

"You also know the lingo so you can snap orders when the right time comes. In other words, you as Ekar, are going to herd me up to chin with the commander and his executive officer. When we get close to them, we take charge. Get it?"

Young Horner frowned, sucked in breath slowly.

"Yes," he nodded. "I guess you're right. We might get away with it, at that."

"We've got to!" snapped Dusty. Then turning to Biff and Curly, "The big job is up to you two. Stick these bums over behind that small ship so they'll be out of sight when the hatches are opened. Then get into the ship and take this mug, Ekar, with you."

"Take him with us?" Curly ejaculated. "Why not plug the rat?"

"Because I've got other ideas!" Dusty snapped him off. "He's the guarantee that you two will get away in case something goes haywire at the last minute. With him aboard, I don't think they'll dare shoot.

"Start the engine once the pontoon touches water, and if things are going O.K., keep the cabin door open. If not, slip the hoisting hook from the inside. The lever's right over the pilot's seat—and get the hell away. You know the job to be done—it'll be up to you then."

As Dusty talked he tried to make his voice sound convincing, but he knew in his heart that he wasn't even getting to first base. What they had already accomplished was child's play compared with the job to come. Yet—there was no other way out.

Someone had to continue on to St. Albans. Ekar's very attitude had increased its mysterious significance. With luck—a carload of luck—all four of them might continue on their way. But Biff and Curly must, and their only hope of success lay in what he and Jack Horner could do.

"Too many chances, that way," Curly broke into Dusty's thoughts. "We started together, and we finish together! The four of us rush them—and the four of us leave in the plane. And that's final!"

"Right!" Biff Bolton echoed. "That's what I'm thinking too. We stick together!"

Dusty gritted his teeth, started to lash into the both, but Agent 10 beat him to it.

"Dusty's right," he said firmly. "Hate to admit it, but he is. It's the only way out. But don't worry, we'll join you two. Maybe we'll have to swim for it, but we'll get there."

With that, young Horner started peeling off Ekar's uniform. A minute or so later he was wearing it himself and standing still while Dusty covered the side of his face with the bandage. Presently Dusty stepped back and grinned.

"Damned if you don't look like twins," he grunted. "Remember, act the part—you know, snarl and curse at me, and all the rest of it. Good."

Turning to the other two, he said: "O.K., the parade's starting. Better bolt this door after we leave. Sit tight and hold your horses—we'll be with you. But in case not, a million in luck.

"Get through to the place someway. Work the C-Ray if you can. If you can't don't let them get it. And give them hell the best you know how. Head for the States if you have to. I've a hunch that they know we're wise to something—and that may delay them. But—O.K., Jack!"

SAVAGELY BRUSHING aside all thoughts except those of the immediate job, Dusty walked over to the side door, twisted the knob and shoved it open. It opened into a narrow, lighted companion-way leading aft toward a flight of steel steps that went topside. He hesitated, felt the muzzle of Agent 10's gun digging into the small of his back, and heard his friend's disguised voice.

"Straight ahead, captain! And I wouldn't try anything foolish if I were you. Pulling this trigger would be a pleasure indeed!"

Even as the voice came to him, Dusty saw a door on the right of the companion-way open and a Black sailor, hands and face smeared with oil, step through. He glared at the man, then half turned his head.

"No need of breaking my back, bum!" he snarled. "I'm not trying anything funny, am I? Hell, I know when I'm licked!"

The Black sailor, who had paused to watch them, slid his lips back in a smirking grin. Dusty continued to glare at him, and walked past. As he did he heard Jack Horner bark something at the man in his native tongue, and heard the man reply in kind. A moment later, a steel door slammed shut. Then Agent 10's hand gripped Dusty, and jerked him to a half halt.

"Your guess was right," came the faint whisper. "All hands are at their stations. Only the commander and executive officer are in the control-room. To the right at the top of the ladder. Don't worry about that mug. Bawled him out for leaving his post. Okey! Up we go!"

A gentle push sent Dusty forward. He grasped the latter and started up. It came out into a small companionway that he judged to lead toward the forward part of the conning tower. As he passed the second door on the right, the gun jabbed his back.

"In here, my friend! And keep your hands up!"

A junior officer passing across the end of the companionway caused Jack Horner to snarl the words. Dusty obeyed instantly. Then when the other reached around him, grasped the knob and shoved open the door, he stepped inside. His first impression was that of stepping into a cupola of half steel bracing and half heavy plate glass ports. Through the plate glass ports he faintly saw the outline of the bow of the submarine cutting through grey-green swells. Then, two figures bending over chart tables, straightened up, made hissing sounds with their lips. Cruel eyes, slightly fogged with annoyed wonder, bored into Dusty's face. He returned the look blankly, and walked toward them.

"Halt, Captain Ayres! Stand right where you are!"

Dusty stopped at the sound of Jack Horner's voice, tensed his body and watched his pal out the corner of his eye. The Intelligence man had his free hand to the exposed side of his face. He took two steps forward, clicked his heels, and started to say something in Black Invader jargon.

But he cut it off in the middle and slapped his gun up and over in a movement quicker than the eye could follow. Dusty saw the start of the motion, and knew that it was the signal. And even as Jack Horner's gun barrel crashed against the sub commander's left temple, Dusty had crashed into the executive officer and was smashing him down onto the steel deck. A muffled roar came from the man's lips, and was cut off sharply as Dusty drove his clenched right fist into the man's neck.

Getting up on one knee, the Yank pulled his own gun free, took careful aim and smacked it down on the Black's skull. The man, who was weakly pawing at his neck, gave a little grunt and went limp as a dish-rag.

"One for our side!" came Agent 10's excited whisper. "Just watch them a second. Be right back!"

Before Dusty could say anything, young Horner turned and disappeared through a side door. He was back in the matter of twenty seconds, grinning with grim satisfaction. At Dusty's questioning look, he jerked a thumb back toward the door.

"Radio-room," he said quietly. "Thought of it on the way up. He won't bother us. And I locked the other door on the inside. Now, keep down, so you won't be spotted from the forward deck. If anybody knocks on the door, let them in and smack them. Here's where I prove my navy training. Hope to God I get the expressions right!"

Taking a position over by the door through which they had entered, and keeping down below the level of the heavy plate glass ports that looked out onto the forward deck, Dusty watched breathlessly as Jack Horner grabbed the "Stop Turbines" signal handle and shoved it down.

ALMOST INSTANTLY the tremor of power that had been rippling through the craft ceased, and forward motion started slowing down. After casting a quick look forward, young Horner moved over to the side panel covered with signal speaking tubes that connected with all parts of the boat.

For one suspense-tingling moment he studied the copper plates over each speaking tube, and the Black Invader inscriptions upon them. Presently he selected one on the far right, jabbed the signal button under it, and snarled sound into the tube. A few seconds ticked past and then a couple of short grunt-like sounds came from the speaker unit fixed to the top of the panel. At that moment Agent 10 turned his head toward Dusty, grinned and nodded.

"Ordered hatches up for plane hoisting," he whispered. "The deck officer is reporting here. Better, that way. The other slobs won't be expecting orders from him. Get set!"

Dusty answered with a quick nod and pressed back against the wall. The forward motion of the submarine had stopped entirely now. It was simply nosing gently into rolling swells. From the forward deck came faint sound of voices—voices obviously barking orders. Dusty wanted to move forward and look through the glass ports, but he forced himself to remain right where he was. His job was to take care of all "visitors."

Suddenly, there came a sharp rap on the door. Jack Horner, staring through the port did not turn, but Dusty saw his body stiffen. The knock was repeated as Dusty reached for the knob with his left hand.

In his upraised right hand he held his gun. Twisting the knob he pulled the door open and pulled it toward him. A figure stepped quickly inside, clicked his heels and started to salute. But he never finished the salute.

In a lightning-like movement, Dusty shoved the door shut, and at the same time brought down his gun. A low whistle of air rushed through clenched teeth, and the newcomer collapsed in Dusty's arms. He lowered him gently to the deck.

"O.K.!" he hissed softly. "What's happening?"

"Hatches opened!" Agent 10 whispered back without turning. "Plane coming up now. It—"

He cut it off short with a curse, leaned closer to the glass port. Dusty could restrain himself no longer. He leaped forward, peered cautiously through one of the other ports.

The launching crane had swung the plane clear of the side of the submarine. Those in the plane had cranked the wing sections forward into place. But the craft was dangling twenty feet above the water, and on the deck of the submarine a dozen Black sailors were staring at it as though in a trance.

Directly down in front of the port through which Dusty stared, the Black who operated the launching crane was making no effort to lower the plane into the water. As a matter of fact, he was leaning out of the small forward door of his compartment, and was pointing toward the plane and yelling something.

"That rat—on the crane, Jack!" husked Dusty. "What's he saying? Damn them, why don't they put it down?"

Jack Horner groaned aloud. The groan mingled in with his words as he dragged Dusty back from the port.

We're sunk, Dusty! That bum is the one we met in the corridor below. Out of sixty men he would have to operate the launching crane. He's telling the launching crew something is wrong. He's saying that he's going to swing the plane back over the hatch!"

"The hell he is!" snapped Dusty, spinning toward the door. "Come on—we'll rush them! Our only chance!"

Jack Horner said something, but Dusty didn't hear it. Gun clenched tightly, he was already out the door and racing down the companionway to the crane-winch room. Slamming open the door he piled inside. The figure leaning out through the forward hinged door that looked straight out onto the bow deck, jerked back in and turned.

It was impossible for Dusty to clear the mess of gear on the floor and reach the man. So he simply squeezed the trigger of his gun. He saw the man throw up his hands and drop. But that was all.

The instant his gun barked he hurled himself across the small room, tumbled into the operator's seat and threw down the pulley lever handle. Gears whined, and the plane squashed down into the water. Slamming on the winch brake to stop slack cable from piling down on the wing, Dusty shot a quick glance back, saw Jack Horner at his heels, and then leaped over the dead Black and tumbled out onto the forward deck. Like statues of frozen marble, half-a-dozen Black sailors, lining the port rail, stood gaping at him wide-eyed.

"Let 'em have it, Jack!" bellowed Dusty, and flung up his gun.

Gun spitting flame and sound, he raced across the deck, straight for the gaping Blacks. Two of them screamed, flung up their hands and went spilling head over heels into the water. The rest sprang into action, and went scuttling toward the shelter of the upraised hatch covers.

"Jump!" came Biff Bolton's booming voice across the twenty-odd feet of gray-green water. "We'll make the bums pull in their necks!"

Through a blurred haze Dusty saw both Biff and Curly leaning out through the cabin door. Each had a gun, and both were sending hot steel zipping across the forward deck of the submarine.

Half turning, Dusty grabbed Agent 10, lifted him clear of the rail and threw him bodily into the water. Then he dropped flat, rolled over twice, until he was behind an anti-aircraft gun mounting. Using it as a shield, he emptied his gun at three figures trying to climb out through the now opened conning tower hatch. Screams blended in with his shots, and three heads dropped back out of sight.

"Come on, kid! For God's sake, come on!"

Curly's voice blasted against his ears above the crackle of a machine gun from the aft deck of the submarine. Unseen steel wasps twanged against the hatch covers to his left. Dropping his empty gun, he braced himself for the fraction of a second, then leaped across the open part of the deck and hurled himself over the chain rail and down into icy cold water. Breath clamped in his lungs he struck out blindly, and only stopped and shot his body to the surface when his hands touched metal.

He came up right beside the pontoon. Directly above him a gun was cracking out sound and flame. Through water-blurred eyes he saw the head and shoulders of Biff Bolton. The big pilot was lying on his stomach, half out of the open cabin door, and reaching down with his long arms.

Bracing himself with one hand Dusty lunged upward with the other. Steel fingers grabbed his wrist and held fast.

"Not now!" he choked. "Taxi—taxi away—take off!"

Hardly had the words left his twitching lips than the idling engine roared into life, and an icy whirlwind smashed against Dusty and tugged at every inch of his water drenched clothes.

Foam swirled around his body as the plane went sloshing forward, and spray, like tiny barbs of steel, cut into his face. But with teeth clenched and eyes closed he managed to fling up his free hand and hook it around one of the pontoon struts.

AND THEN began an ordeal in hell itself. Everything became a whirling blur of chilled crimson. Invisible hands seemed to grip every part of his body and pull in opposite directions. And all the time a frozen cloud of thundering sound engulfed him. But presently, that part of his brain still able to register reaction, told him that he was being slowly pulled upward; that steel-strong fingers were hooking under his armpits, and lifting him clear of icy depths.

The next thing he realized he was slumped down in a seat of the plane, and Biff Bolton's ham-like hands were slapping both of his cheeks.

"Hang on, skipper! Everything's swell now!"

The booming voice cleared Dusty's brain like a curtain being pulled aside from a sun-flooded window. He stared into the grinning face bending over him.

"Thanks to you, Biff!" he grunted.

"Aw shucks!" Bolton waved it off. "If it hadn't been for you, I guess none of us would be here."

Dusty only half heard him. The plane was streaking up for altitude toward a heavy cloud layer. Curly Brooks at the controls was busy getting every ounce of speed out of the engine in the nose. Behind in the left rear seat Agent 10 was binding up a bleeding left arm. And beside him, grinning happily, was Biff. Ekar, however, was nowhere to be seen. As that realization came to him, Dusty sat up straight.

"The rat?" he asked. "Where the hell—"

He cut it off as Jack Horner stopped fixing his arm long enough to point down back toward the water.

"Jumped out as we were pulling you aboard!" he grunted. "Left me this souvenir. But I think his own guns on the sub got him. Dived right into a burst from that aft machine gun. Didn't see him after that—Curly had the ship underway."

Dusty nodded and said nothing. Gritting his teeth against the cold that still held his whole body in its freezing vise, he stared moodily at the loud layer above. The miracle of miracles had taken place. The four of them were free, and in the air again. And now, what, he asked himself.

As though the whole thing had been actually timed to the split second, Curly Brooks turned toward him.

"So what, kid?" he echoed. "Which way after we hit the clouds? Those bums will radio to hell and back now."

"No they won't!" Jack Horner cut in. "It will be a damn cold winter before they'll get that set in shape. I smashed all four tube blocks when I crowned the operator."

The Intelligence man's words lifted a great weight from Dusty's shoulders. It also sent a tingling warmth through his goose-pimpled body.

"Boy, you do think of everything!" he grinned at young Horner. "Without the radio it'll be hours before they can contact anybody, and then it won't matter a damn to us. They'll have to find us first. Curly, head her straight for the English Channel as soon as we're in the clouds."

"Nix, wait!" barked Jack Horner. "I've been thinking. We wouldn't have a chance, Dusty! Hell, where will we get fuel? The X-Twelve was to do that job! Tell you what—get me to the French coast and leave me. Then head back home. There's no sense in all of us running into more jams. Our big plan is out, now. And—"

"And pipe down!" Dusty cut him off. "Hell, do you think we came this far, just for the ride? Nothing doing, we go through as is. Now listen—here, Curly, I'll take her!"

"You'll take nothing!" Brooks rapped out. "Sit down, you're rocking the boat. What were you going to say?"

Dusty, who had half risen from his seat, shrugged and slumped back.

"I was going to say," he continued, "that we can carry on the bluff we started. If it worried Ekar, it's a cinch that it will worry others. Enough, I think, to get them out of the way long enough for us to get in and do something."

"Biff!" growled Curly, half turning. "Did this guy bump his head as you pulled him in? What the hell are you raving about, Dusty? What bluff?"

Dusty paid no attention to the remark. He went on addressing his words to Jack Horner.

"When Ekar left those mugs guarding us that time," he said, "it's my guess that he went up to the radio-room to send some kind of a message about the French coast and airplane carriers—about the plane carriers in particular. Now here's my idea—you've smashed their radio, so they can't use it. Good! You can still play the part of Ekar, and use the radio on this crate. Get it?"

Young Horner half frowned, then opened his eyes wide.

"You mean—"

"Sure!" Dusty barked without giving him a chance to finish. "Using their lingo you can call an S.O.S. Emergency to all air stations, and order them to maintain a strict watch for American carrier squadrons reported off the west coast of Ireland.

"Report them anywhere, it doesn't matter. The idea is to get the bums hunting for the advance planes of Yank carriers. We're in a Black ship, so we'll just join the hunt, drift through them and have a forced landing near St. Albans.

"There's a dozen lakes around there where we can sit down. Then that way, you and I won't have to risk going down by chute in broad daylight. Think you can do it?"

"The signaling part, yes," grunted the other. "All dot-dash

code is from ground stations, so I can say that I'm aloft. But supposing the message we believe Ekar sent out, wasn't about our carrier bluff? Suppose it was something entirely different?"

"So much the better," Dusty came right back. "You're spreading this new alarm—just got it from prisoners, see? And you're heading north to help in the search. Hell, it's perfect. That way, they'll even be expecting this crate."

"Listen, here's another idea!" Curly Brooks broke into the conversation. "Why not, instead—"

"Hey! The blinker light!"

Biff Bolton's shout was a waste of breath. They all saw the red signal light on the radio panel start blinking. In a flash Dusty shot out his hand, slapped on contact, and turned the dial knob. He was three quarters of the way around the dial before sound came crackling out of the speaker unit.

With a yelp Agent 10 suddenly started crowding into Dusty's seat.

"Move over, move over!" he hissed. "Let me get at the set!"

Dusty obeyed automatically, one half of his attention on the Intelligence man's flushed face, the other half on a queer series of unintelligible signals coming from the cabin speaker unit.

"What? What's up?" he choked out.

Agent 10 was busy getting a finer tuning on the incoming wave-length signals.

"Plenty!" he breathed fiercely. "That's a powerful ground station trying to pick up the submarine we just left. Shut up, all of you. Going to try and get it on our wave-length, direct!"

141

CHAPTER 11
PLAN G

FOR A full half minute Jack Horner worked feverishly at the radio panel. Presently he grunted and snatched up the transmitter tube. The other three saw his lips part, and heard crisp phrases in Black Invader lingo clip out.

Instantly the signals stopped coming from the speaker unit. In a few seconds they began again, much clearer and sharper in tone. Dusty knew from the grin that curled back Jack Horner's lips, that the signals were now coming in direct.

Then followed two minutes of rapid-fire conversation between Agent 10 and the operator of the unseen ground broadcasting station. And then the Intelligence man shot out his hand, snapped off contact and slapped the transmitter tube back on its hook. The grin he turned on Dusty stretched from ear to ear.

"Did you by any chance plan this with the Blacks, and not let us know until now?"

Dusty gaped at him.

"Huh?" he got out. "Plan what?"

Jack Horner jerked a thumb at the radio panel, chuckled.

"That was their main coastal station at Southampton," he said. "Ekar called them to report our capture and to give the carrier bluff warning. Told them to check-back with him in an hour for further information. That's what they were doing. So I confirmed the warning in Ekar's name, and requested that all available air defenses be sent out at once to patrol all areas four hundred miles off the Irish coast. And—"

"You did? Oh boy—"

"Shut up! Here's the news! They asked if I thought it advisable for the fleet to steam back into the great circle course, and inform H.Q. to delay Plan G for twenty-four hours. And I said, yes! And with true Ekar authority, if you get me!"

"The great circle course?" murmured Dusty. "Plan G? Now, what the hell could that mean?"

"Don't know," Agent 10 said excitedly. "But it may mean this—the attack we expect is to be launched via the great circle course. A direct line, get it? And it must be coming by air, else why keep their boats off the great circle course?"

"Right!" agreed Dusty. "Keep the path, of attack clear below. Why? Because it might destroy anything under it—I'll bet my shirt on that! Remember Ekar's chemical bombers? If one of those, for instance, happened to tumble down on a fleet of navy ships—get what I mean?"

"That this bird, Ekar, has more of them damn things over on this side of the pond, you mean, skipper?" Biff Bolton's rumbling voice broke in.

"Not that exactly," Dusty shook his head. "I don't know what they've got. Just guessing—guessing that it's something that they want their own navy ships to keep clear of. There's the answer to what your dad said, Jack—about not even a Black rowboat being sighted for the last week.

"They've withdrawn them all back to Europe, cleared them away from the American coast. Why? Because this damn Plan

143

G might possibly destroy their own navy by accident! So they're taking no chances, and keeping it out of the way. By God, we've got to go through now. Curly! What's our position?"

Curly bent forward and squinted hard at the instrument panel, leaned back again.

"Make it about six hundred due east of St. Nazaire," he grunted. "Maybe I'm wrong fifty miles either way. Don't think so, though."

Dusty glanced at his wrist watch, saw that it had stopped, and looked at the dash clock. The radium hands pointed to sixteen minutes after seven.

"Should make it in at least two hours and a half," he murmured, more to himself. "Just in time for breakfast. Curly! Take her up to fifty-five, and set her dead-on for London. We're going to town."

"Okey," grinned Curly and nosed the plane skyward.

Settling back in the seat, Dusty had started to map out a plan of attack when Biff leaned forward and shoved something into his hand.

"Speaking of breakfast, skipper," he rumbled. "Have some. Took it off them mugs before we pulled out."

Dusty glanced down at the bar of concentrated sweet chocolate and chuckled. Biff was also handing a bar to both Curly and Agent 10.

"Thanks, Biff," came from Curly. "I get it! A swell idea, too!"

Bolton frowned, scratching his head.

"Huh? What do you mean?"

144

Curly took a bite, waved what was left toward Dusty and Jack Horner.

"Keep their mouths full, and they can't talk," he said. "Then you and I can do something about this air tour!"

Dusty turned to young Horner, gestured hopelessly.

"Your dad was right about it being a good idea to form a nit-wit squadron," he said. "Remind me, when we get back, to suggest Lieutenant Brooks as C.O."

"Thanks, pal!" snapped Curly, shaking his head violently. "But I'm damned if I'm going to cheat you out of your just rewards. You've proved yourself capable of that task. And I refuse to stand in your way. Right, Biff?"

"For the first time, since I met you, yes!" mumbled Bolton with his mouth full.

And so it went for the next hour, each poking fun at the other; kidding, razzing, anything to make conversation and thereby keeping their minds off what was to come. For an hour it lasted, and then each of them lapsed into grim silence and battled with his own particular thoughts.

The plane on even keel at fifty-five thousand feet, plowed steadily northward, now bathed in the glistening rays of the morning sun, and now totally engulfed in blurred, swirling cloud mist. Though not a word was spoken, all four of them, at some mutual inner signal stiffened slightly in their seats and fell to maintaining a relentless vigil of the surrounding sky and clouds.

A hundred different times one or the other of them started violently in his seat, raised his hand to point ahead or to the side, only to drop his hand with a grunt as he realized that the patrolling planes he believed he had sighted were only wind-whipped cloud specks in the distance.

It was Dusty who eventually broke the tensed silence. He reached over and touched Curly on the arm.

"Let me take over, kid," he said quietly. "I know the London area pretty well, you know. Learned it during those exchange courtesy maneuvers with the British."

Curly started to object, then shrugged and changed seats.

"Guess you do at that," he grunted. "Oh well, maybe I'll get honorable mention when the whole blasted thing is over. But, just for memory's sake, what's the exact plan when we get there?"

"If we do!" Jack Horner echoed.

"We will, don't worry!" Dusty snapped back over his shoulder. "But we've got to work together, strange as that may sound to you, Curly. So first, explain the operation of this C-Ray focusing unit, Jack, will you? All of us had better know how to operate it."

"Right," nodded the Intelligence man leaning forward. "It's simple. See that box on the floor to the left? It contains six C-Ray recording cells. That panel in the middle of the dash is the focusing plate.

"On the left, here, these six sets of throw switches and rheostats serve as the control for the cells. There is a throw switch and rheostat for each cell. Use them one at a time. Not all at once, or you'll simply get overlapping pictures on the plate.

"First you throw the switch, and allow a few seconds for those black glass vacuum tubes, extending down from the panel plate, to become heated to current strength. Then you turn the corresponding rheostat knob. Cook says that you must turn it way around to the stop peg, at first. Then you gradually ease it off to a point where you get maximum clearness in the recorded picture."

"And what if you turn one on and get nothing?" asked Curly. "What's that mean?"

"If you get nothing, it means that the recording cell has been damaged," replied Agent 10. "If you get a solid black that seems to ripple, it means that the recording cell is where it cannot trap sufficient light rays. Like it was in my pocket, and I hadn't placed it anywhere yet. Look, I'll show you. They're in that box, so we'll just get rippling black. Dusty throw that top switch!"

REACHING OUT his hand, Dusty flipped down the tiny throw switch, then rested his fingers on the rheostat knob beside it. A faint high-keyed hum seemed to fill the interior of the cabin, and all eyes fixed on the black glass tubes extending down from behind the focusing plate saw the first one on the right glow faintly with a sort of phosphorescent sheen.

A moment later Jack Horner nodded.

"Okay, Dusty, start turning."

Forefinger and thumb gripping the knob, Dusty turned it all the way around to the stop peg, then started to slowly turn it in the reverse direction. Meanwhile his eyes were clamped on the recording plate.

Its surface, which had been a frosty grey in the morning light, changed to a deep black, and tiny parallel threads of light started moving across its surface from right to left. The movement of the lines was so slow and so perfectly synchronized that the black seemed to ripple rather than the threads of white to move.

"See?" Jack Horner grunted. "We get nothing because the cell is in the box where there are no definite light ray waves to be recorded. It's—my God—something's coming through!"

It was true! The threads of light moving across the surface of the focusing panel had merged into a shifting conglomeration of shadows. A few seconds and the shadows stopped moving; became stationary and took on definite shapes and outlines. Yet it was impossible to see anything clearly; it was like looking through a light-blurred film negative. Something was there, but much too indistinct for the human eye.

"The knob, Dusty!" came Agent 10's hoarse voice. "Turn it back slowly!"

Dusty was already twisting the knob back in reverse. Suddenly a clear picture took form before their eyes. It was the picture of a steel-walled room; rather a steel-walled compartment. In the very center, its hull keel resting on a padded cradle, was a small low wing, two-place coastal amphibian. It was a Black Invader Navy plane, and climbing in through the hull hatch door was the figure of Ekar!

For seconds not one of those watching Yanks even so much as even breathed. Spellbound, they stared wide-eyed at a picture which sent memory racing back over two short hours, back to the forward plane compartment of the bogus submarine X-12. For it was a picture of that compartment now being recorded on the focusing plate.

Where their plane had been, now rested the coastal amphibian. Hoisting tackle had been fitted to the ring atop the cabin. The wings were still folded back, so that the plane would clear the hatch sides on up-hoist. And Ekar, head re-bandaged, body clad in a Black Navy uniform, was climbing into the pilot's cockpit.

The door dropped shut behind him, four Black sailors came into the picture, and as they placed their hands against the folded wing, the craft moved upward and disappeared off the top of the focusing plate. And the picture became one of just a steel-walled submarine plane compartment, with the Black sailors walking out of view.

"Ekar! Then he didn't die! Wasn't hit after all!"

As Agent 10 mumbled the words, he shook his head and blinked his eyes stupidly, like a boxer who has been left-hooked down on the canvas for the count of nine.

But the sound of his voice seemed to free the other three from their paralytic trance. With a smothered curse, Dusty leaned over, and jerked up the lid of the box clamped to the left side of the cabin floor.

Wadded cotton batting met his eyes. He dug both hands into it, probed them about and pulled out, one by one, five objects of wired metal, each about three inches long, an inch square, and containing at one end a disc of what might be, but wasn't, crinkled and dried rawhide. Just five, only. There were not six.

Holding them in his hands, he switched his eyes to Jack Horner's face, started to speak but stopped as the Intelligence man's mouth dropped open, and his eyes went wide with sudden understanding.

"Hell yes, hell yes, of course!" he gasped. "I remember now—was examining one at Baltimore Base—heard your plane—shoved it in my jumper pocket. Hell yes!"

"And when you changed into Ekar's uniform, you took off the greaseball jumper!" ejaculated Dusty. "It must have rolled out of the pocket—and nobody saw it. God, it's back in that sub now!"

Dusty absently put the C-Ray cells back in the box and shut the lid.

"There goes everything out the window!" grunted Curly Brooks. "You didn't bust that crate's radio, by any chance Jack?"

"No," answered young Horner thickly. "I didn't, of course. And now that bum will send out a general warning. He knows where we're headed—knows we're headed for St. Albans. Oh my God!"

"Well, it's a break in a way!" Dusty cut in savagely. "But for that bit of luck, we might never have known. Might have slammed right into their reception committee. So we'll fix that, right now!"

"Huh?" the others chorused. "Fix what?"

Dusty didn't answer. He reached out and flipped on radio contact, tuned up full transmission volume and spun the wavelength dial knob to the official U.S. Navy S.O.S. Emergency reading. Then he grabbed the transmitter tube.

"All navy stations stand by!" he bellowed into it. "S.O.S. Emergency call. Captain Ayres forced landing at AT-Thirty-seven. Engine crippled, and repairs impossible. Send help at once to AT-Thirty-seven. Craft is captured enemy navy plane. Send help at once—at once—at once!"

The last he made weaker and weaker, and then cut off contact right in the middle of a word. At the same instant he thumped down on right rudder, slammed the stick over and sent the plane racing around toward the east.

"Hey!" Curly barked as the motion of the plane threw him momentarily off balance. "Call your shots, will you? And why east? AT-Thirty-seven is southwest of us! Didn't you know that?"

Dusty gave him a hard look.

"No?" he grated. "Nuts! Figure it out, sweetheart. Don't you suppose that will be picked up by the Blacks?"

And before Curly could answer, "Sure it will," he went on. "Maybe by Ekar, if our luck is still with us. I'm counting on two things. One that they'll go highballing way the hell down there to nab us. And the other, that they'll be so excited that they won't think of checking on their directional finders until it's too late. That's why I'm heading east, to get out of the way, just in case."

SILENCE SETTLED over the group as Dusty stopped. There wasn't anything to say now. The situation was more or less in the lap of the gods. If Ekar had intercepted the S.O.S. call, or even if his friends had got it through to him, and he went racing far out to sea on a goose chase, so much the better. If he didn't—well, there wasn't much of an answer to that.

For twenty minutes Dusty flew steadily eastward, then, face

lined grimly, he eased back the throttle and started nosing down through the clouds.

"Keep your seats, gents," he grunted out the corner of his mouth. "If I'm right we're around Dunkerque. I'm going down to check. Give me a hand on the position checking."

Steepening his dive, Dusty shot the ship down almost vertically, but flattened out sharply as they bored through the last of the clouds and came out into shadow-flooded air. In spots, though, the sun was breaking through, and it created more than enough light for them all to see what lay directly below.

One long look and Dusty knew that he had been wrong—but only by a matter of a couple of hundred miles. They were over the entrance to the English Channel, about halfway between Cherbourg and the southern coast of England.

Once he'd learned his exact position, he began a minute inspection of the air below. Far to the left he saw a V formation of Black Invader defense scouting planes. They were headed in a southwesterly direction. Below and straight ahead, the southern strip of England spread back to the northern horizon like a squared crazy-quilt pattern.

But as far as he could see, there was not a single plane in the air above it. True, the seaplane base east of Southampton was well-planned. He could see half a hundred amphibians and coastal planes riding at anchor inside the breakwater. And outside the breakwater a double-strength flotilla of Black destroyers. But they, like the planes, were not in motion.

Casting his eyes to the right he stared at the coast of France and Belgium, with its many brownish-black blotches, signifying where the gods of war had struck during the Black Invader conquest of Europe.

In the Channel more Black ships were to be seen. As a matter of fact it seemed as though the entire Black naval force had returned to drop mud-hooks in Anglo-French waters. But there was not an airplane to be seen in the air. Perhaps there'd be plenty inland, up north toward London, but down there at the British water gateway there was none on patrol.

Had Agent 10's fake order, or his own S.O.S. call, been successful?

The question burned through Dusty's brain as he allowed the plane to flat-glide toward the southern coast of England. An answer to the question was not to be had at the moment. He could only guess from what he could see that the answer was yes. But yes or no he wasn't going to turn back, no matter what happened. Crazy? Perhaps. Time alone could prove that.

Opening the throttle, he eased the ship up into the lower cloud layer, flew blind for a short time, then gradually worked the plane up through to the crest of the layer.

A thousand feet above was another cloud layer; a thick one that blotted out the burning rays of the sun striving to pierce it, and made the passageway between the two layers seem as an endless, murky corridor leading across the heavens to nowhere.

Flying by electro-magnetic compass, Dusty held the ship headed for invisible London, and hunched grimly over the stick. For no reason at all, tiny fingers of ice started rippling up and down his spine, and he caught himself glancing nervously in all directions.

Try as he would, he could not kill a sudden eerie feeling that something was going to happen. Something totally unexpected. He cursed softly, tried for the thousandth time to rid his mind of the taunting thought. But it still clung to him.

And then, without warning, the unexpected did happen!

Far off his right wing there was movement; blurred movement streaking down out of the upper cloud layer. It zipped for the lower cloud layer, then suddenly arced up and swung around toward him. And it was then that he saw it clearly. It was a sleek, low-wing coastal amphibian. More than that, the very amphibian he had seen registered on the C-Ray focusing plate!

CHAPTER 12
MYSTERY BELOW

"**C**URLY! MAN the aft gun! Here comes trouble!"

Even as he cracked out the words, Dusty slammed the ship over and around on wing-tip, and slid both thumbs up to the electric trigger trips on the stick. The amphibian, with Ekar obviously at the controls, was boring in like a streak of black light—thundering recklessly toward them as though he were determined to crush them into oblivion by the very impact of mid-air collision.

A hard grin on his lips, Dusty held his own plane dead-on for the other. Nose to nose attack was old stuff for him. Let the other guy take the bit in his teeth if he wanted to. There was always plenty of time in which to go to work.

"Get him, skipper! Get him!"

Biff Bolton's voice rumbled in Dusty's ear. He chuckled harshly.

"Had an idea something like that myself," he grunted. "Keep clear of those cabin windows!"

The last word had hardly died to the echo when the stream-lined snout of the amphibian's hull spat jetting flame, and invisible fingers dug grooves along the sides of the pontoon.

"Nerves, eh?" shouted Dusty, as he yanked the plane to the left. "Well, don't blame me because you're a bum shot! Gave you first crack didn't I?"

With that he flopped the ship over on its right wing and came tearing back in. Ekar tried to meet the attack nose to nose, but hot steel from Dusty's guns twanged off the hull snout, and started creeping up to the cockpit windows. That was just a wee bit too close for the Black and he whipped into a quick half-roll.

The maneuver was mistake number three, for as the amphibian started over and down, Dusty cut around in a half circle and flattened out. The result was that Curly, manning the aft cabin gun, couldn't have missed even if he had shot snowballs. But he wasn't shooting snowballs. On the contrary, it was singing steel that raked the amphibian from end to end, and shattered the port side cockpit window into splintered nothingness.

"Got him, kid!" shouted Dusty. "Good work—you got him!"

And it certainly seemed to be the case, for the amphibian wobbled crazily out of its dive, skidded off to the right, and then lurched drunkenly into a spin. As it started down the second time, Curly plastered it some more. The effect of his shots was uncertain for the amphibian spun down out of sight in the lower cloud layer.

The instant it disappeared. Dusty cut back toward the north, put the nose down just a hair, and went thundering forward.

"Hey, I haven't finished!" came Curly's bellow. "Poke her down while I make certain. Just warming up!"

"Nix!" Dusty snapped. "You did plenty, lad. And it's up to us to get out."

"But why?" Brooks argued heatedly. "You don't know for sure!"

"Right!" his pal agreed. "But we can't risk showing ourselves below the clouds. Don't you get it? Us tearing down will mean a scrap to those on the ground. They'll add two and two and get the right answer. But him smacking up by himself can mean most anything to them. And he's going to smack, damn him! See the way he flopped into that spin? He'd been hit, kid, hit plenty!"

Curly growled something that Dusty didn't get, but made no further attempt to argue. And for several minutes, a good twenty minutes in fact, the only sound inside the cabin was the faint throbbing beat of the engine in the nose. Then, finally, Dusty hauled the throttle all the way back and sent the ship coasting down in a wide gliding turn.

"This is it, fellows," he said quietly, trying to keep the excitement out of his voice. "Jack, come up in this seat along side of me. Curly! You and Biff keep down out of sight. No telling whether we'll run into any patrols."

Leaning forward in order to spot the ground scene at the

earliest possible instant, he sent the plane cutting down through the last cloud layer, and came out into clear air.

"Right on the nose this time, anyway!" he grunted to himself.

And right on the nose it was. Below and directly ahead was the northern fringe of the St. Albans area. Beyond it, southward in the distance, the famous Hendon air terminal. Rather, what war had left of it—a barren, black and gray blotch on the ground. And beyond Hendon, the once mighty city of London.

GREAT SECTIONS of it had withstood the ravages of war. But most of it, stretching to the four points of the compass, was shell-gas and flame-scarred ruins—a silent, terrible tribute to the courage and fighting spirit of Britons who had valiantly defended their all against overwhelming odds until the very ground upon which they stood, back to back, was blown out from under them.

"Look—down there to the left!"

Jack Horner's startled cry jerked Dusty's eyes away from the blood-freezing panorama that was London. He followed his friend's pointing finger, looked down and saw three or four miles to the east of St. Albans a large square of ground that from his altitude seemed to be dotted with gigantic beehives. Set in parallel rows of four to a row, five rows in all, were great dome-shaped buildings. They were almost like astronomical observatories, except that they were situated on billiard-table ground instead upon hills and mountains.

Flanking them on all four sides were long, oblong buildings of the store-house and troop-barrack type. And set back even farther, on the south side, was a series of squatty buildings that gave the appearance of extending down into the ground. As for windows in the squatty buildings, there was none. The oblong buildings, though, were full of windows. And the beehive structures appeared to have a crack in each, running from the ground up to the peak on the west side.

"That's the answer!" came Agent 10's hoarse whisper. "That's the answer, right down there!"

"Yeah," grunted Dusty, ruddering a shade to the right. "But I sure can't read it from up here. What do you suppose those things are? Look like new-fangled bridge caissons to me. Only each of them seems to be split."

Agent 10 seemed not to hear. Face drawn taut, he sat staring downward at the queer scene. A second or two later, though, he sighed audibly.

"Look at those troops patrolling the whole place!" he breathed. "And those air patrols to the east. God, Dusty, I don't under—"

He let his voice trail off. Dusty made no comment. He too had seen the ant-like figures that were Black troops patrolling the entire area. And also, the V formation of Black ships drifting about in lazy circles far to the east. But he had only given them a glance. What interested him the most was a small lake right close to the war-shattered village of Hertford, and not more than seven or eight miles from the guarded area.

Swarms of brown-clad figures were at work on the northern side of the village. One guess and he knew that he was right. The brown-clad figures were English prisoners being forced to do reconstruction work. He could see squads of Black troops keeping guard.

Without turning his head, he called to Curly.

"Change seats, kid!" he said. "And listen, all of you! At last I've figured out a plan that will click. Jack, I'm your prisoner, see? An English prisoner—say a spy you picked up farther north. You're flying me down to see the big shot, Mlada. Important information, see? Biff, you keep out of sight. Curly, you land us on that lake down there—over by that busted-up village.

"Get her in close to the shore. Keep your pants on, no matter who shows up. Jack, you keep me covered with your gun—we go ashore, start heading for St. Albans. With that officer's uniform of Ekar's you have on, we can plow right through and maybe commandeer one of those cars I see down there.

"Now, Curly, once we're landed, taxi out into the lake. You know, waiting for your superior to come back. Give us five hours. If we're not back, take off for an hour and come back and do the same thing all over again.

"But all the time keep trying these C-Ray cells. And if you see anything that makes sense, gives you a good idea of what's going on here—then never mind about Jack and me. You take off and head for home. You'll at least have enough fuel to take you within reach of one of our Atlantic destroyer squadrons.

"Now, one more thing—if you get into trouble, either waiting for us on the lake, or in the air, the last thing you are to do is smash this C-Ray stuff. Right, take over now. Jack, get set—look the part.

"Biff, keep down out of sight. Your face is clean. Curly's, here, is so smudged up, damned if he doesn't look like a Black from a distance. Curly, get that greaseball cap down lower, and hide them golden locks. And keep it that way."

As Brooks changed seats he was struggling for words that wouldn't come. It was Jack Horner who spilled them out.

"You're crazy, Dusty! It will never work! Put me ashore alone! That's the only hope we have!"

"Don't be a fool, Jack!" Dusty snapped. "You've got to have reason for picking this particular spot. I'm the reason—a valuable prisoner you want to rush through to Mlada. Alone, you might be questioned. But with a prisoner anyone we meet gets the idea at once. They know why you're headed for the forbidden area."

"Maybe," murmured young Horner. "But—"

"No buts about it! Hell, it took us long enough to get here. So let's go into action and cut the arguing. Here, you take three of these recording cells, and I'll take two. We'll place them when and where we can. But, C-Ray cells or no C-Ray cells, we've got to get inside there and see what the hell is what!"

"And Biff and I just suck our thumbs!" growled Curly as he swung the craft down lower to the lake. "Nuts! I don't like the looks of it either way. Too easy, for one thing."

"And that's our one hope!" Dusty retorted. "It looks so easy that the bums down there won't even stop to figure it the other way."

"I'd feel better if I knew Ekar was fish food!" mumbled Curly. "And—oh hell, you always did get your own way. But be careful, you big slob. And pin it in your hat—Biff and I aren't going to wait until we grow beards! Well come after you!"

160

"Check!" Bolton boomed from his place on the cabin floor.

Dusty grinned, but said nothing. There was nothing to say, now. Out of a thousand different plans of operation that had come to him, since first he talked with General Horner, the one he had just outlined seemed the only one that held any hope of success.

True, it could be knocked full of holes, and a million different upsets could kill it in the bud. It was similar to walking into a lion's cage and punching him right smack on the nose. The lion might leap and claw you to shreds. And then again, the lion might be so surprised that he'd beat a hasty retreat to think it over.

What Jack Horner and he intended to accomplish hinged on that very same angle of performing the ridiculous. No sane man would punch a lion on the nose. And neither would a sane man float down before the very eyes of enemy air patrols, land on troop-infested enemy ground, and walk brazenly right through the whole works. It just wasn't being done. Right! So stick with us Lady Luck while we do it!

"God, I hate to do this. But here we go, damn it!"

AS THE half-groaned words rippled off Curly's lips, he flattened the glide to within a few degrees of stalling speed and let the ship float down toward the placid surface of the small lake that was now less than five hundred feet below. Body tensed, nerves held in an iron grip, Dusty stared hard at the right shore.

It was fringed with trees that straggled back into open fields, and finally a road a quarter of a mile, beyond. As far as he could see no figures were running toward them from the war-ruined village of Hertford. However, he was too low down now to tell for sure. And what the hell did it matter, anyway? He'd be seeing plenty of Blacks soon enough.

Swi-i-ish cr-r-ump!

Under the skillful guidance of Curly's hand the plane touched water and mushed forward. Goosing the engine just a bit he put on right pontoon rudder and nosed toward the shore. A minute or so later the nose of the pontoon was bumping gently against the muddy bank.

"You first, Jack," said Dusty in a low voice. "Some one may be watching. Don't forget, act the part. Right! So long fellows!"

The two left in the plane made no comment, but the long silent look they gave both Dusty and Jack Horner spoke more than words possibly could. Instinctively Dusty reached out, gripped them both by the arm, and squeezed hard.

"Come ashore, dog! At once!"

Jack Horner's grating voice cracked from up on the bank. With slow, deliberate motions, Dusty climbed down onto the pontoon, ducked under the prop blade that Curly had switched off, and climbed up on the bank. But before he straightened up, young Horner's voice snarled at him again. The Intelligence man pointed with the gun he held in his hand.

"Go down and push the plane clear!"

Then in a louder tone he bellowed something in Black Invader jargon. What it was, Dusty didn't know. But he could guess. Jack was playing his part for all it was worth—and for any opened eyes and ears that might be about. In other words, he was probably instructing his aerial chauffeur to wait.

As a matter of fact, after Dusty had climbed down and shoved the pontoon nose clear of the bank so that the plane drifted outward, Agent 10 confirmed his surmise.

"Said that I might be a long while and for them to wait until I showed up," he whispered softly, at the same time training his gun on Dusty. "Added that I'd boil them in oil if they let anyone try to commandeer the plane, and that they were to talk to no one. Maybe that will help them. Okey, walk a couple of yards in front of me, and keep your hands half raised. God, I hope you're right."

"We've got to be!" Dusty hissed back, with considerable emphasis on the first word.

And with that he started walking through the scraggly growth of trees that fringed the lake. With each step his heart seemed to bang all the harder against his ribs.

For a crazy, insane moment he had the almost uncontrollable desire to laugh. It just couldn't be true. He and Jack doing lockstep across enemy countryside—enemy countryside three thousand miles of water away from home. Hell, it was an absurd dream. Such things happened only in books.

"Heads up! Here's the first hurdle, kid!"

Plowing forward, for the moment completely lost in his whirl of dizzy thoughts, Dusty almost missed Jack Horner's low-voiced warning. He raised his eyes and looked ahead.

They were crossing the last field, and were about thirty yards from the twisting dirt road that lead in the general direction of the St. Albans area. Coming up the road from the other direction, from the village of Hertford, was a low-slung infantry patrol guard car, containing three figures. The two, who sat in front, were ordinary soldiers. But the solitary figure in back had the appearance of being some kind of an officer.

Dusty breathed a silent prayer that the officer was not of too high rank—and not too inquisitive either.

"Your plan wasn't it?" he grated at himself. "Thank yourself for what happens."

"Halt!" Jack Horner's voice snapped out sharply.

Dusty stopped, a dozen paces from the road, and assumed a bitter and dejected air as his pal, quite evidently covering him with the gun, stepped boldly out into the center of the road and held up his free hand.

THE BRAKES of the oncoming car screeched sound and the car slithered to a stop a dozen yards in front of young Horner. The figure in the back seat climbed out and came stalking forward. He was an officer, all right, but evidently of low rank, for he clicked his heels and saluted Jack Horner. Then he said something in his native language, meanwhile turning cruel eyes on Dusty. Young Horner replied in the same tongue, with just a faintest sneering lilt in his tone. For several moments they continued the conversation. Finally the Black officer saluted again, half turned and motioned the men at the car wheel to drive closer. The car rolled forward and stopped. Bowing stiffly to Jack Horner, the Black officer jabbed a finger at Dusty, then motioned him in back. A sickly grin on his lips, the Yank ace slouched forward, climbed in and dropped back on fee cushioned seat. No sooner had he settled himself than Jack got in and sat beside him.

Slamming the door shut, the Black officer snapped something at the two men in front and waved them out of the car. Then he slid in behind the wheel, meshed gears, and sent the car rolling forward.

Slouched down in the corner of the seat, Dusty squinted at Agent 10 out the corner of half-closed eyes. The Intelligence man was turned toward him, looking at him with a sneering expression. Suddenly, he laughed harshly.

"Well, my dog friend!" he leered, "a few minutes more and you shall have the doubtful pleasure of meeting your swine countryman face to face. We are going there now. It is what you call in your cursed language, the perfect break—for us!"

The emphasis on the two last words, and the faint tightening of the lids of Jack Horner's eye, hidden from the driver at the wheel, was like a bolt of electricity ripping through Dusty.

CHAPTER 13
MLADA!

WHAT WAS the hidden meaning behind Jack Horner's sneering words? Face to face with a countryman? Going there now?

The questions burned through Dusty's brain as he turned a surly expression on his pal. The answers might mean most anything, if he could only guess them. But he couldn't, and staring into the Intelligence man's face didn't help in the least. Snarling triumph stared back at him.

Yet, inside, Dusty knew that something had happened. Something not on the calendar—something that was a perfect break for them. To be forced to remain silent, and to act a part he didn't feel in the least, was like rubbing salt into already festering wounds. There was nothing else to do about it, however. The car was racing full out toward the St. Albans area. Already they were passing large groups of Black troops. The Black at the wheel was sending them jumping for safety with the wailing siren. And not more than a mile or so ahead Dusty could see the tips of the queer domed-shaped buildings, surrounded by troop quarters.

As though he were Fire-Eyes, himself, the Black at the wheel charged right past a dozen different guard patrols, shouted something at them that Dusty didn't understand, and kept right on going. The sudden and almost unbelievable change of events set Dusty's blood to tingling, and the inside of his mouth became very dry.

In a hazy sort of way he had figured that it would take Jack and himself a good two hours to bluff their way through the guard lines, and even get within striking distance of the mysterious area. But here they were going right smack into it—like a couple of war lords riding back from great victories to receive the acclaim of the multitudes. And acclaim it seemed to be, for the nearer they came to the secret area the more those they passed on foot took notice of them. Some of the groups even waved field service caps and broke into loud cheers.

Not daring to even look at Agent 10, lest the driver suddenly turn and see the questioning look he couldn't keep out of his eyes, Dusty slouched lower in the seat and gazed straight ahead through narrowed lids.

The car had now slowed down a bit and was rolling along a paved street that paralleled the rear of one of the large barracks. At the end it turned the corner and started across the flat-squared area containing the five rows of beehive buildings.

For the moment, Dusty forgot about the cockeyed situation and peered hard at the buildings. They were spaced about a hundred yards apart, and although the car was traveling down the middle between two rows, he could see them in detail. They were apparently built of, steel-reinforced concrete.

The base of each was flush with the ground. In fact, it seemed to be sunk into the ground. On the eastern side was a nine—or ten-foot opening. The opening was made by a sliced section being removed and rolled back to rest against the adjoining section of the dome-shaped affair.

Inside, everything seemed dark. But as the car rolled past the third one, Dusty caught the glimpse of what looked like a large steel ring—more like a steel collar that flanged outward from the center. What it was, what it was meant for, was impossible to tell at the distance.

"They interest you, eh? Perhaps you will see more of them later!"

Jack Horner's harsh, grating tones jerked Dusty out of his wondering reverie. It was then that he realized he had unconsciously leaned forward and was gaping open-mouthed at the beehive buildings. At about that same moment, the Black at the wheel turned around, smirked at him, then looked at Jack

Horner and said something in his native tongue. Young Horner laughed loudly, nodded his head as though agreeing, and rapped out some answering sentence.

Body a mass of coiled springs, ready to fly out in all directions at most any moment, it was all Dusty could do to keep a dejected look on his face. The car was now barely creeping forward through crowds of Black soldiers craning their necks to get a better look at him.

The wailing siren and the snarling echo of the Black at the wheel had very little effect. To Dusty, it was almost like mushing through a sea of ugly, triumph-twisted faces. And what in the name of God was it all about?

Over and over again the question pounded through his head, beat against his brain with the nerve-shattering monotonous beat of perpetual rain upon an upturned face.

Finally, he shoved his crazy thoughts into the background of his brain. The oar had plowed through the last of the soldiers. Rather, armed guards had swept the soldiers out of the way and enabled the Black at the wheel to slide up to a stop in front of a small building on the far side of the squared area.

Leaping out, the Black officer stepped back, pulled open the rear door and smiled at Agent 10. Returning the smile, the Intelligence man got down to the ground, and jerked his head at Dusty.

"Get out, my friend!" he snapped. "Follow this officer. But be careful. I shall be right in back of you!"

Dusty hesitated the fraction of a second, saw no enlightening glint in Jack Horner's eyes, and got out of the car. Head bent, he followed the Black officer through wide doors down a short foyer, up a flight of stairs, and along a corridor to an ornate carved door before which a guard stood at rigid attention.

With a flick of his hand the Black officer waved the guard to one side and rapped on the door. A moment of waiting and the door was opened and a second guard stuck his head outside. He stiffened as he saw the Black officer, gaped as his eyes switched to Dusty, and swallowed hard when he finally saw Agent 10. But at a snarling command from the Black officer, he came out of his trance and flung the door open wide.

THE ROOM into which Dusty stumbled, as Jack Horner pushed the gun into his back, looked like a combination business office and radio station. The right wall was covered with instruments, and a Black soldier, earphones in place, was sitting in front of the main panel.

The other three walls, including the one with the door, were lined with file; cases. At the rear center of the room was a massive U-shaped desk. Sitting behind it was a small man with a head so big it seemed a miracle that his thin scrawny neck was able to support it.

The general arrangement of the room Dusty took in in one flashing glance. It was the figure behind the U-shaped desk that instantly caught and held his attention. Never had he seen a face quite like the one before him now. One eye was half closed and contained a copperish glint, while the other was wide open and an icy blue.

The nose started to hook at the bridge, then changed its mind and became almost button-shaped at the end. The upper lip was thick and puffy, but the bottom lip was so thin that it seemed to recede into the mouth. Yet, notwithstanding, the jaw was large and squarish.

The ears, one slightly larger than the other, were so flat against the side of the pear-shaped head, and so completely hidden under shaggy black hair that there seemed to be no ears at all.

But perhaps, the most startling thing of all was the tint of the skin. It wasn't just one tint. The cheeks were copperish, the forehead a brownish yellow, and the lower part of the face a sort of muddy chocolate.

The face of faces startling, as a whole, and inexpressibly repulsive in detail.

"So, you're Mlada, huh?"

Dusty didn't realize he had blurted out the words, until the figure behind the desk jerked up to his full height of about five feet three inches, leaned forward and bored him with his weird eyes.

"Yes, I am Mlada!" he said in a voice that sounded like marbles rattling around in a tin can. "And to see me is to meet death!"

Dusty shrugged.

"All right," he said. "So I—!"

He cut it off sharp as Jack Horner's gun dug into the small of his back.

"Silence, dog!" thundered his pal. "Yours will not be the first swine English carcass I have placed a bullet in!"

English! The word rasping off Agent 10's lips made Dusty start inwardly. So! He was not Yank, but English? He shrugged, looked scornful.

"Right-o!" he said quietly. "Sorry!"

A moment or two of silence filled the room, and then the one called Mlada spoke again.

"Here is a piece of paper, and a pencil," he said, pushing both forward on the desk. "You will write down the names of the other leaders of your little organization. Five, we know—and with the exception of one, they no longer exist. You will now give us the names of the other leaders."

Dusty looked from the man's face down to the paper and pencil, back to the man's face again.

"I don't know what you're talking about," he said with rising inflection. "And even if I did, I wouldn't think of doing what you ask. I'm English, you know—a Briton!"

The hairline eyebrows of Mlada arched upward, and his thick, puffy upper lip wrinkled.

"British, and therefore stubborn!" he said. "You know nothing about the organization of English prisoners which is working secretly against us? Nothing at all, eh? Very well, we shall see. Perhaps we can make you recall a few things to your fading memory."

The Black jabbed a thin thumb at one of a row of buttons that circled the entire inner edge of the desk. Almost instantly the door opened and the guard outside stalked stiffly in and saluted twice as stiffly.

Mlada snarled something at him, and he retreated, only to reappear a couple of moments later leading a man, the very sight of whom made Dusty's blood boil with rage. The new-comer was obviously English, even though his civilian clothes were in shreds, and his well-featured face battered and bruised. It was his carriage, the way he held his head up and gave Mlada a straightforward, quiet, defiant look, that stamped him true English at once.

"As I told you," Mlada sneered at him, jerking his head toward Dusty, "we have caught another of your fool comrades in our net. Soon we shall have them all!"

FRANK BLUE eyes looked into Dusty's face in an expressionless stare. In the split second allowed Dusty tried to read some hidden warning. But there was nothing to read, and then the Englishman looked back to Mlada.

He seemed on the point of speaking, but suddenly tightened his lips to a thin line and remained silent. Mlada's face flamed with anger for a moment, then he broke out in a harsh laugh.

"You both should be in the theatre!" he bellowed. "You are born actors—but very poor spies! So you will not tell me who the others are?"

The last he spat out at Dusty. The Yank ace glanced sidewise at the Englishman, but the other was looking calmly at Mlada. Then Jack Horner's gun pressed against his back.

"Write them, my dog friend!" came his words. "It will be best for you. And do not try to fool us by making them up!"

A signal? Dusty took a chance, nodded and stepped to the desk and picked up the pencil.

"Very well," he said. "I am rather fond of my precious hide, you know!"

"You rotter! Blast you!"

The Englishman shouted the words, and would have leaped

at Dusty had not the one guard in the room grabbed him and pulled him back. Dusty half smiled.

"Sorry old thing," he murmured. "But everything's too much of a beastly mess, don't you think?"

The officer tried to talk, but he was so choked up with blind rage that he simply sputtered. Mlada laughed again, fixed his sneering eyes on Dusty.

"Your comrade does not possess your good sense," he said in his marbles-in-a-can voice. "Perhaps, for this, we will not kill you as we planned. Now—the names, and where they are to be found!"

Dusty bent over the paper to hide the expression he knew must be on his face. He was positive that Jack Horner had signaled to him. Signaled to him to fake the names—make them up. For what? To gain time?

He could feel the back of his neck crawling, and his fingers gripping the pencil were all thumbs. He knew that every eye was riveted on him. Names? Yes, he could make them up. But writing where they could be found; that was different. He might put down a place Mlada would know instantly was wrong.

The thoughts tumbling through his mind vanished as he sensed that Mlada had suddenly stiffened. He jerked his eyes to the man's face. It was twisted with rage—a sort of frozen rage. Then came Jack Horner's voice.

"Step back, kid, to the right! Quick!"

Automatically, Dusty did so. Something was shoved in his hand. It was a gun. He gripped it, jerked his head around. At his side stood Jack Horner, balancing lightly on the balls of his

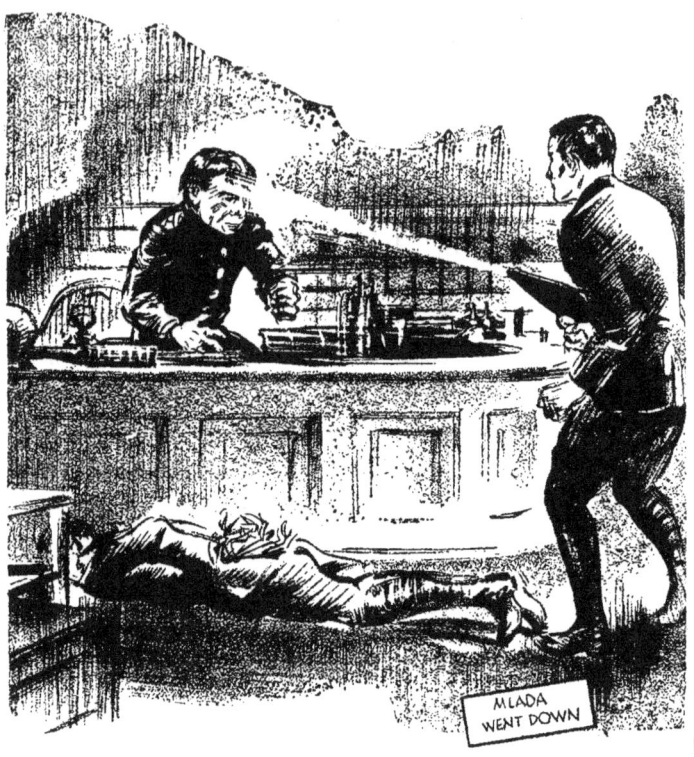

MLADA
WENT DOWN

feet, his eyes darting from figure to figure in the room. And in the Intelligence man's right hand was a Black Invader gas gun.

"English! Take that guard's gun—back over to us!"

The Englishman blinked, opened his mouth to speak, but snapped it shut. He grabbed the gun away from the gaping guard, and backed over to Dusty and young Horner. Shoulder to shoulder they stood facing four pairs of startled, hate-filled eyes; the eyes of the guard, the Black officer, the radio-man, and Mlada.

For perhaps five seconds no one moved a single muscle. Then Jack Horner broke into a low chuckle.

"Remember Agent Sixteen, Mlada?" he shot at the tensed figure back of the desk. "Remember Agent 14, Agent 12, and God knows how many others? But perhaps you did not know them by their numbers. It doesn't matter anyway. Stop—don't move your hand!"

Mlada's right hand, creeping toward the half circle of buttons, froze. Jack Horner smiled, slid his eyes to the Black officer who had driven the patrol car.

"And you need not try to reach your gun," he said. "I have it, you see! You were too interested—didn't even know that I'd taken it. And by the way, never take a man at his word in time of war. The one you expected to meet will be very disappointed! All right, all of you, get down, face to the floor, and clasp your hands behind you. Dusty—you too, English, on your guard!"

Choking back useless questions, Dusty covered the radio-man and the guard, motioned them to go flat on the floor. They hesitated just a split second, then dropped down. The Black officer took longer, but he went down quicker as the Englishman calmly slapped the gun barrel down on his head—Mlada, however, did not move. Like an ugly statue he sat rigid, weird eyes blazing into Jack Horner's face. Dusty started toward him, but stopped as the Intelligence man shook his head.

"This, for the moment, is personal, kid," he shot out the corner of his mouth. "You two watch the others, and the door."

As he talked he walked close to the desk.

"Our first meeting, Mlada," he said in a deadly voice. "Somehow I never really believed that I would meet you. You were a myth to most of us—a rotten, hell-born myth. But I am meeting you at last, and as I look into your murderous face I recall a lot of things.

"I see brave men dying like flies. I see them tortured and

maimed. I see innocent women and children ground into dust under your iron heel. And they, all of them, Mlada, are crying out to me from their unknown graves, crying out to me to give you your reward!"

Never before had Dusty heard the deadly, almost inhuman note, in Jack Horner's voice. The Intelligence man's face under its make-up tinting had gone chalky, and save for his hand holding the gun, every part of his body twitched convulsively. It was as though the man had suddenly gone stark, raving mad. Impulsively, Dusty took a half step forward.

"Jack! Hold—!"

"Shut up! This is my affair!"

Agent 10 didn't even turn his head as he rasped out the words. He kept his eyes fastened on Mlada, who now was seemingly shriveling up inside.

"At last I meet you, Mlada—Mlada, the murderer of brave but helpless men! Mlada, the slaughterer of women and children! Well—it is to be no more! The fires of hell are waiting for you—with this gun!"

With a movement faster than the eye could follow, Jack Horner stepped back one pace. In the same instant Mlada whipped his hand to the row of buttons. But he never touched them. A thin stream of purple spewed out from Jack Horner's gas gun, and caught the Black full in the face. A gurgling grunt spewed from his lips; he half raised his hands, as though fending off a blow, and then, with a rasping sigh, fell over sideways. His body hit the end of the desk, bounced off, and crumpled down on the floor in a lifeless heap.

CHAPTER 14
ZERO HOUR

HAD THE roof suddenly caved in at that moment, Dusty wouldn't have even noticed it. Nor the Englishman either, for that matter. Like a couple of cigar-store Indians, they stared unblinking at the limp form on the floor. Finally Dusty found his tongue.

"Well, that's one less!" he managed to gulp. Then at Jack Horner who stood transfixed over the body. "Out of it, Jack I Snap out of it! Got to move fast!"

The sound of his friend's voice served to break the spell that gripped the Intelligence man. He turned and nodded.

"Right! I'm all right. Sorry—maybe I should have waited. But—damn his heart! It's better this way!"

Leaving the men on the floor to the Englishman's care, Dusty walked across the room and flung an arm over his friend's shoulders.

"I understand, kid," he said quietly. "Would have done it myself if I'd had the chance. Now buck up. I want some answers—no, wait a minute."

He turned, looked at the only door leading into the room. The Englishman guessed his look.

"It's pretty thick, Yank," he said quietly. Then added, "You two are Yanks, aren't you?"

Dusty simply nodded, turned back to Agent 10.

"Better make this private, Jack," he said. "When I open the

178

door a crack, yell for that mug outside to come in. You know, in his lingo, of course."

Jack Horner nodded, waited until Dusty crossed the room, and eased open the door a crack. Then he shouted something. Instantly the door was pushed open wide, and the guard stepped inside, stopped short and gaped. Then he stopped gaping as Dusty's gun came down on his skull, and the door clicked shut.

"Getting good at that sort of thing," grinned Dusty, catching the man and lowering him to the floor. "Makes it two in a row. O.K., the first question, Jack: what the hell is the show we've been staging?"

Agent 10 had become his old self. He grinned, gestured with one hand.

"As I said in the car," he grunted, "it was the perfect break. That bum the Englishman crowned was expecting a Black agent and a prisoner. Expecting him by car, though, not by air. However, he seemed to take it as a matter of course, and told me he'd take us to Mlada.

"That got me excited—gave me an idea, too.

"It was worth the risk to go straight through to Mlada. Hell, the thing was perfect. He told me that Mlada had another prisoner. Who, I didn't know. But when he said that Mlada wanted you to face him—well, it seemed too good to be true. He was going to take us right through to Mlada! Me, close to Mlada, and with a gun in my hand! God, I wanted to laugh in his face. But I didn't, of course, and simply went through with it, and tried to tip you off."

"I had that hunch," nodded Dusty. "But you sure gave me some dizzy moments."

"Couldn't do anything about it," young Horner explained. "As a matter of fact the stage was set. Nothing else to do but see it through. Why I waited when we got here, was simply to find out about this man you were supposed to face.

"Then, when they brought English, here, into the room and concentrated on you two, that was my chance to get this tramp's gas gun and finish the act. But damned if I wouldn't have risked others' hearing the shot of an automatic, and plugged him anyway. He had to die—damn him, he had to!"

"Quite right, old thing," the Englishman said quietly. "He was the world's worst rotter. A dirty killer if there ever was one. And though you may not realize it, you've performed a very great service to your country, though, I'm afraid that there are others who can carry on with the devil's plan—unless we do something about it."

"Unless we do something?" echoed Dusty. "Hell, that's what we're here for! Listen, you know anything about a G Plan? Has it got to do with those beehive things out there? What in hell is this place, anyway?"

"You might call this place the beginning of the end of civilization," replied the Englishman without the slightest trace of emotion in his voice. "A G Plan? Sorry, but I haven't heard of any G Plan. But I fancy it has to do with the Paralysis Gun turrets out there, which you term beehives."

"Paralysis Gun?" yelled Dusty. "What kind of a gun is that?"

"The name applies more to the shell loading than to the gun

itself," said the Englishman. "Each gun, mounted under those turrets, can hurl a rocket shell a distance of over thirty-five hundred miles. Now don't look so amazed! It's quite true.

"To supplement gun-barrel velocity, each shell has its own rocket projection force. Before the original force is spent, timing mechanism brings the rocket force into play, and an additional thousand to fifteen-hundred miles is thus gained. Oh, I assure you that it's quite all very true. For several weeks, this dead devil here, has thoroughly enjoyed himself by not only explaining to me, but partially demonstrating, the whole devilish thing in detail. You see, I was one of the first to find out what they were up to, here in this area. But unfortunately for me, I tried to hinder their progress and was captured along with a few others. The others were—killed eventually."

"And why not you, too?"

Dusty wanted to bite his tongue off for having asked the question. The Englishman paled, gritted his teeth. "Lord knows I wanted nothing better than to join them!" he said bitterly. "But the devils refused to permit me to die. They suspected that I was—"

The man stopped short, suddenly bent over and cracked his gun barrel down on the heads of the guard and the radio-man. As they both went limp, he straightened up and continued talking as though he had only paused to tie his shoelace.

"They suspected that I was one of the leading figures of an organization working to rearm, and perhaps some day rise up and hurl off the steel yokes they have put around us. They were correct in that. But they were blasted fools to even dream I

181

would so much as raise a little finger to help them in their bloody work."

NOT ONCE as he spoke had the Englishman so much as raised his voice, or gestured a single point. His words had been calm and his tone level. But their effect upon Dusty and Jack Horner was correspondingly doubled. His country soaked in native blood from one end to the other; his relatives, friends and fellow countrymen dead or feeling the iron heel of the barbaric conqueror, this man was quietly proving himself the very soul of courage and grim, dogged determination. Impulsively, Dusty put out his hand.

"Sorry, English," he said. "I didn't mean it that way."

For the first time the Englishman smiled.

"Naturally not," he said. "I was simply stating my own position. But, er—er, things have been happening rather fast. Just how did you two chaps get here?"

Dusty grinned.

"Got the tip something was wrong. So we came over to find out."

"From the States?" gasped the Englishman incredulously. "Good Lord!"

"We'll give you the details when we have more time," Dusty went on hurriedly. "Other things to do first. Now you say that those guns out there can shoot around thirty-five hundred miles? But there are only twenty of them! What the hell do they expect to do with twenty guns?"

"Quite a bit," replied the Englishman with a grimace. "As I said, each gun shoots a rocket shell. Now by a very delicate timing mechanism the shell can be made to fall apart in sections high above a certain area. And—"

"Fall apart?" echoed Dusty. "You mean spray shrapnel thirty-five hundred miles away?"

"Oh no! The loading of the shell is a highly concentrated gas compound. It is a thousand times heavier than air; it is invisible and odorless and it paralyzes all human form of life. The effect is instantaneous once it is breathed into the lungs, and the effect lasts for a minimum period of twenty-four hours.

"In other words, the turrets out there can be revolved so that the guns can be brought to bear on any section of ground within a thirty-five hundred mile range. The idea, of course, is simply to make it possible for the Blacks to maintain control of any and all captured countries.

"They simply bombard an area where there is trouble—the trouble-makers are rendered helpless and Black troops pour in and quell the disturbance before it can flare up again."

As the Englishman paused for breath, Dusty got in the question uppermost in his mind.

"But how about gas masks?" he said. "Why couldn't the populace wear gas masks until the bombardment was over?"

"They could," the other observed, "if they knew where and when the bombardment was to take place. They'd only have to wear the gas masks for ten minutes or so—the paralyzing qualities of the gas becomes nil within ten minutes after it settles to the ground.

"But that is the rub—there is no advance warning, no exploding of shells in the air. You don't know that it is upon you until it is too late. And—by Jove, I think I know what the G Plan is all about.

"It must be the bombardment of the entire eastern area of the U.S.A. He, Mlada I mean, told me that soon your country would be captured, and without a single bit of resistance. Yes, that must be the G Plan. Even if we could warn your countrymen, it wouldn't do much good!"

AS THE Englishman stopped again, Dusty and Agent 10 exchanged meaning glances.

Why had there been no action along the Canadian front? Because the Blacks were waiting for the moment when they could storm right down without even firing a shot!

No wonder the Black navy had been withdrawn from American waters, and from the great circle course. It would be too dangerous for them to remain under the path of the phantom shells, for fear that some of them might function prematurely and destroy their own ships.

And that general call to all Black agents, that they had picked out of the air? It had been a warning to them to prepare for the secret moment—a warning to leave the doomed areas, or else be ready with masked protection.

Hell, yes, those and a hundred other different things which had happened, all found their origin here in the St. Albans area—here among the paralysis guns.

Impulsively, Dusty reached out and grabbed the Englishman's arm.

"You're sure, of all this—about these guns?"

A bitter smile creased the other's face.

"I'm jolly well positive!" he said. "Part of my entertainment, as a prisoner, was to be a bloody laboratory guinea pig. I, and a few others. By the way, one of them was a Yank, I'm sure. The poor devil either escaped or was killed.

"By God—Sixteen!" cried Jack Horner. "This is what he tried to tell you, Dusty—about these guns!"

"Sixteen?" echoed the Englishman.

"A friend of ours," Dusty put in quickly. "But, listen, what do you mean, a guinea pig? You mean they—"

"Exactly! Our prison is next to the control station, and the experimental laboratory. They tried their blasted gas out on us. A hellish experience, I assure you. Quite a few of the lads died from it. I don't believe they exposed me to it as much as they did the others. Wanted to keep me and wear me down so that I would tell what I knew.

"As a matter of fact, they were quite clubby with me at times—told me and showed me the whole blasted business, then tried to pump me for what I know. Confound the lot of them, I told them where they all could jolly well go!"

Dusty could hardly wait for the man to finish.

"Control station?" he echoed excitedly. "There is a control station for these guns?"

"Of course," nodded the other. "Only two loaders are in each turret, and they wear special suits. The range finding and firing of the guns is electrically controlled. The control station is the ammo stores as well. There is a compressed-air chute leading from the control station to each turret.

"The gas chambers and detonating charges are sent through

the chutes to each gun turret. They are then craned into the loading chamber of each gun, and made ready for firing by the two men in each turret.

"They signal back 'ready to fire' and the control station officer throws the switches for individual fire or salvo fire. A bloody earthquake it seems, too, when the blasted things go off. A week ago they tested the guns, but without gas loadings. Frightful, I assure you."

DUSTY ONLY half listened to the last part. His brain was clicking over at lightning-like speed. A wild, crazy plan had suddenly come to him. He faced the Englishman again.

"The prison is a part of the control station?" he said. "You know the way there from here?"

"Know the way?" the other echoed. "Been driven over it so often I could do it in my sleep. But what the devil of that?"

"Plenty!" snapped Dusty, and grabbed them both by the arm. "Listen, both of you," he went on. "Our only hope is to stop this thing before it gets started. Now if we could capture this control station, their guns wouldn't be worth a damn to them. See what I mean?"

"I fancy I do," nodded the Englishman. "But it's impossible, Yank. We'd pass fifty of the blighters, at least, between here and the control station, and meet another ten or fifteen of them in the place. We'd be dead men in no time. And besides, even if we did take over the place, we couldn't hope to hold out against them for very long."

"Maybe," grunted Dusty. "But we could put their guns on the blink!"

"Blink? Blink?" mumbled the Englishman, frowning.

"Out of commission," answered Dusty. "Those loading tubes—they carry the gas chambers and the detonating charges don't they?"

"Yes! Yes, of course."

"And there are two men in each turret, to receive the stuff? Right?"

"Yes, you're quite right," nodded the Englishman. "For the last week there have been two men on constant duty in each turret."

"Then that means they're ready to let drive at the slightest warning?"

"Yes, I suppose so."

Dusty grinned.

"Simple, once we get charge of the control station," he said. "Detonating charges are controlled by adjustable timing. The lads in the turrets probably do that during loading. Well, we'll time the things ourselves. Say, time them for five seconds—enough time for them to pass through the tubes and out into the loading receiving trays in the turrets. Then, *blam*—the detonating charges blow up, set off the main charge, and the lid pops off hell right in each turret. And twenty long-range guns are so much twisted junk. Am I right?"

"By Jove—by Jove, I fancy you are, Yank! A premature explosion in the turret would be the answer. Bloody right, it would. But, I say old thing, we'd first have to capture the control station you know. Aren't we putting the cart before the horse, what?"

Dusty grinned, looked at Jack Horner.

"Guess you'll have to ride herd on two of us this time, kid," he said. "I mean this—you're taking English and me back to the prison. English can lead the way, he knows it. We'll each stuff a gun in our shirts, and you can—wait!"

Dusty darted over in back of the desk to the rear wall, picked up something and brought it back. It was a portable skirmish machine gun of English manufacture, its circular drum fully loaded. He grinned at the Englishman as he held it out.

"A souvenir that goes back into use," he chuckled, then gave the gun to Jack. "We can do a lot of damage with this when the time comes. Now you just do your stuff. They saw you bring me in, so it won't mean much if they see you herd me out."

"But we won't be going out, old thing," the Englishman spoke up. "We go through the tunnel—it leads from here underground back to the control station, about two hundred yards back. We'll just have to worry about the sentries. Then, they don't know who you really are, eh?"

"Not yet, I hope," Agent 10 said. Then turning to Dusty, "But what about these rats here? If they're discovered, we'll—"

"We'll be well on our way," Dusty cut him off. "Leave them as they are. It's the only thing we can do. No, by God—it isn't. Hell—Curly and Biff! We've got to tell them to be set for a quick take-off. Wait, hold everything. God, I hope they're trying all the C-Ray cells in rotation!" As Dusty spoke he fished one of the recording cells out from under his shirt-front and placed it on the desk so that it focused on Jack Horner.

"Nod your head, Jack," he ordered. "Grin—signal to them to hold the focus." Going around in back of the desk, Dusty jerked open drawers until he found a fair-sized sheet of white paper and a pencil. Putting the paper flat on the desk he went to work. Presently he straightened up, went over beside young Horner and held the paper up in front of him. Printed on it in large letters were the words:

GET SET FOR QUICK TAKE-OFF.
HOLD PLACE IF POSSIBLE.
WILL COME RUNNING AFTER HELL POPS LOOSE.
MEET YOU SOON!

Dusty held the paper up for three full minutes, then backed up against the wall, creased the paper near the top and hooked it over the back of a chair so that it was still within line of the C-Ray recording cell.

"What the devil is that thing?" gasped the Englishman. "And who are Biff and Curly? You mean to say that—"

"Yeah," Dusty checked him. "A couple of lads who'll stick around and take us home. O.K., fellows, let's go. We've wasted plenty of time as it is."

The Englishman frowned, looked as though he were going to ask a million questions, but didn't. Shrugging and mumbling something about never being able to understand Americans, he walked with Dusty to the door and pulled it open.

CHAPTER 15
YANK LIGHTNING

T HE INSTANT they stepped into the corridor outside, Dusty darted a quick look in both directions and heaved an inward sigh of relief. So far, so good. The corridor was deserted.

"O.K., English! Make it as fast as you dare."

The only sign from the other that he had heard was a quickening of his pace. Rather, he lengthened his stride and went down the corridor, turned sharp left at the end, but instead of going down the stairs to the lower floor, he kept right on to the rear side of the building.

And it was there that they met the first Black. A big, ugly-featured man who was striding up and down on sentry post. He stopped instantly, snarled at them both, and then seeing Jack Horner bringing up at the rear, stiffened and saluted smartly. Tense as the situation was, Dusty had to bite into his tongue to keep from grinning in the man's face.

He succeeded, however, and keeping close to the Englishman, he went through a door that led to a narrow flight of stairs, covered over like a grain elevator chute, and finished at the entrance of a dimly lighted tunnel that was about eight feet high and ten or twelve feet across.

At least a dozen smaller tunnels led off from the main one, and before the mouth of each stood an armed guard.

But although he half expected to hear a ringing challenge at most any second, he kept right on moving forward, shoulder to shoulder with the Englishman.

Fifty yards of the tunnel traveled, and not a sound save that of their feet striking the stones, and the clicking of the guards' heels as each one saluted Jack Horner.

It was hell, in a way, that things should have turned out this way. He had counted so much on the C-Ray cells; figured that they would give them the answer and then they could get word back to the States, so that the Blacks could be thwarted. But it had turned out different. All the alarm warnings in the world couldn't help those back in America, once the Blacks started their invisible bombardment. Nor could help be sent over in time. Help? What sort of help? The Black navy and the Black forces in England would have to be smashed aside first. And then—even then it would undoubtedly be too late. The entire eastern half of the United States would be helpless prey to the Black hordes sweeping relentlessly down from the Canadian front.

No! Crazy, insane as it seemed, and was, three men were tackling a job that thousands should be doing. And tackling it because the fate of millions and millions depended upon their success.

Musing to himself, Dusty plodded grimly forward, chin down on his chest but eyes squinting ahead from under frowning brows. He could see the end of the tunnel now. It seemed to open fan-shape and become two wide flights of steps leading up in opposite directions. Why two flights? Where did they lead to?

He absently toyed with the two questions. And then, suddenly, it happened.

From the rear of the tunnel in back of them came the eerie, blood-chilling wail of a siren.

Three guards, the last three in front of them now, spun half around, fingered their rifles nervously and cast frowning inquisitive looks down the tunnel. Impulsively, Dusty half raised his hand to his shirt front, where nestled his gun. But he caught himself in time and half turned his head toward Jack Horner.

"What the hell's that, bum!" he exclaimed.

"Close your mouth, you bloody fool!"

The words hissed off the Englishman's lips, but Dusty hardly heard them. Ears ringing, he waited, heart in his throat, for his pal to pick up the bluff. It came almost instantly.

"March straight ahead, swine!" young Horner snarled. "And you, too, you English dog!"

OUT THE corner of his eye, Dusty saw the Englishman stiffen, look perplexed for a split second, and then relax. None of the three guards were paying any attention to them. They were still staring down the tunnel. And then Dusty and the Englishman were past them, and at the bottom of the double flight of stairs.

Far back along the tunnel a harsh voice was shouting. In a quick movement Dusty slid his hand into his shirt front, curled his fingers about the butt of the gun hidden there. At the same time he leaned toward the Englishman.

"Quick, English!" he hissed softly. "Which way—left or right?"

"Left!" the other replied. "But we're bloody fools. That was the alarm siren. The whole lot of the devils will be on our necks in no time. They've probably discovered him—Mlada!"

"Left?" he echoed. "Keep moving—follow me! Get hold of your gun!"

It was instinct, more than judgment that made Dusty leap up the steps toward the door on the left. What he'd discover beyond it, he had no idea. Nor did he care at the moment. The Englishman was faltering, not because of lack of courage, but because his physical resources were at a low ebb.

Weeks of unspeakable torture as a prisoner in Mlada's charge had reduced him to the shell of his former self, and instant, blind action, necessary now, was beyond him. He was like a drunken man stumbling forward in the wake of a human tornado. And a human tornado Dusty had become.

He went up the steps like a streak of light and virtually hurled himself at the door at the top.

It groaned from his efforts, then the catch slipped free, the door swung open and he went flying inside. He got a flash glance of a short passageway that opened up into a room shaped like a half circle.

There were many things in that room, but he didn't notice them at once. The only thing he saw at the moment was a Black soldier swinging around and tugging at his holstered gun. The man didn't even get the flap loose. Tearing forward on the dead run, Dusty shot from the hip. The Black went limp, swayed crazily on the balls of his feet, then fell over.

Gun out in front of him Dusty leaped over the prostrate

form and charged out into the half circle room. It was something like a train yard round-house cut in half. The back wall was straight, and from this wall the rest of the room fanned out to form the half curve of a circle.

Along the curved wall was a row of what looked like the loading chambers of submarine torpedo tubes. The heavy disc door of each one was open and swung out at right angles to the wall.

From each opening a set of narrow-gauge tracks led back to converge at a turntable platform at the rear wall. And on each set of tracks, and a foot or so from each of the openings in the curved wall, was a small truck containing five or six metal drums so arranged that the whole looked like a solid cylinder about two feet thick and perhaps four-and-a-half to five feet long.

One sweeping glance took in all that as Dusty skidded to a halt on the corrugated metal floor. And then he saw the human tableau near the rear wall. Eight figures in dirty, grease-smeared overalls were seated at an oblong table. A few of them clutched grimy cards, while the others simply clutched the edge of the table, and sat paralyzed, wide unblinking eyes riveted on Dusty's sudden entrance.

For a good four seconds not a man of them so much as moved. Then like thunder low down on the horizon, muttered rumbling spread from lip to lip, and two of the figures half rose from the bench upon which they sat.

Crack!

A slug of singing steel zipped out from Dusty's gun and

buried itself in the leg of the man nearest him. The man howled with pain and flopped back on the bench.

"Reach up, rats!"

DUSTY'S COMMAND was as sharp as the sound of his gun. For one hellish split second he dully wondered if they understood English. They did. At least they understood the gun in his hand. To a man they raised their great muscle-bulging arms above their heads.

"God, Yank, careful! This place is full of explosives and gas shells. You'll blow us all sky-high!"

The Englishman's voice snapped against Dusty's ear-drums.

"Yeah! Maybe you're right. But keep your gun on them. Jack! O.K. back there?"

"For the present," came young Horner's voice behind him. "But I saw them piling down the tunnel. And Ekar was leading them!"

Dusty almost spun around to stare at his pal. He just caught himself in time. Ekar! Hell, Curly had been right again. The rat had got down O.K. And he was here, now. Curly, Biff—had they—?

He cut off the thought savagely, jabbed his gun at the eight figures at the table.

"Stand up, slow!" he barked at them. "Face the wall—in a line!"

Their movements proved conclusively that they did understand English. Each man got to his feet and then slowly turned and faced the wall." Dusty took a couple of steps toward them.

"Jack! Guard that door! Spray anyone who tries to open it.

195

English, come with me. Get to the left of the line. I'll start at the right. The barrel of your gun just behind the right ear will do the trick. Anyone who moves, gets the trigger!"

Face grim, eyes agate, Dusty walked over to the line of figures against the wall. And then with cold, calculated movements he belted the first and second Blacks behind the ear. They dropped like a couple of logs and lay still. The third and fourth performed the same act. But the fifth started to turn, bring down his hands and snarl. But he never finished the snarl.

Dusty's gun was just about seventeen times faster than the man's movements. He took the blow square on the temple and went down to join his mates. By that time the Englishman had dealt with the remaining three. But not quite.

One of them was struggling to get up from the floor. The Englishman stared at him, half raised his gun. Dusty didn't wait for him to finish. He bent over quickly and belted the man across the side of the head.

"God, Yank—they were unarmed, you know!"

Dusty took a split second to meet the Englishman's eyes.

"Right!" he snapped. "And so are about twenty million American women and children these rats would help gas into Black slavery! Forget it! Give me a hand shoving this stuff into the chutes. Figure that setting the detonating charges for five seconds will be O.K.?"

The other gulped. Things were going just a little bit too fast for him. He was not exactly used to made-in-America methods.

"Er—er, no," he finally got out. "Fancy that a ten second

setting would be better. But wait a tick. No sense in us asking for it. Wait!"

As Dusty started to frown the Englishman ran over in back of the table where the Blacks had been sitting, and stooped over out of sight for a few seconds. When he reappeared he was carrying three gas masks and auxiliary back tanks.

"Seen the blighters wear these," he said, handing Dusty one. "Some of the blasted stuff might leak out. No reason we can't try to live, you know!"

"One for you, English," Dusty grinned, pocketing his gun and slipping the shoulder harness over his head. "Thanks."

The Englishman nodded coolly, went over and gave one to Jack Horner. He was on his way back when there was the roar of voices beyond the heavy door through which they had entered. The door shook violently on its hinges. Jack Horner, who had placed the machine gun on the floor and was struggling into the gas mask harness, tried to stoop down and snatch up the gun. But the harness checked his movement, he stumbled and fell heavily on his side.

WITH A wild curse, Dusty leaped forward, crashed into the Englishman, who was in his path, sent the man flying and reached the machine gun. Half-crouched on the floor, he jerked up the gun, aimed blindly and pulled the trigger.

The gun banged and jumped in his hands, but through the glass eyes of his gas mask he saw the center of the door spit splinters. And a split second later heard piercing howls of pain beyond.

By then, Jack Horner had struggled into the harness and was

tearing the gun from his hands. Through the anti-gas speaking vent in the mask came his muffled voice.

"Hurry up—I'll hold them!"

Dusty didn't reply. He simply nodded and raced back toward the curved wall. The Englishman was already there, and was pushing the first truck forward on the track so that its U-shaped front end was flush with the lower lip of the opening.

And then with his hands he shoved the segmented cylinder off the U groove in the top of the truck and into the loading chamber of the chute. As he did, Dusty reached forward and started to turn the detonating timing knob on the flat end of the rear drum. But the Englishman knocked his hand aside.

"Load them all first!" came the muffled words from out of the gas mask. "Can close all doors—same time. Extra five seconds will give us time to set them all—and release together."

As the man spoke he pointed toward the far end of the curved wall.

On the wall just beyond the last chute was a panel upon which were two multiple gear levers. One, he realized instantly, was for closing all the chute locking doors at the same time, and the other for releasing air pressure in the chute simultaneously.

By that arrangement it was possible to keep feeding gun loadings to all of the twenty turret guns at the same time, so that no turret crew would be held up during concentrated salvo fire.

And the extra five seconds? The time which the two of them would have to set twenty detonating time settings and get the doors closed! Five seconds in which to barricade themselves against any explosion back-firing in the chutes!

Even as the thought flickered across Dusty's brain, he was working feverishly with the Englishman, rolling the trucks flush with the loading chambers of the chutes, and shoving the paralysis gas drums and detonating charges into place.

Twelve of the damn things loaded—thirteen of them! His whole body was drenched in sweat. It was as though he were working inside a Mast furnace. The Englishman was just a hulking shadow weaving and twisting at his side, crashing into him every now and then as he slipped on the steel floor, or tripped over the truck tracks.

Fifteen loaded! Five more to go! Hell, there were more than twenty—there must be twenty thousand! Was Jack holding the rats back from the door? Damn, would they ever get these cursed things loaded?

The crazy cockeyed ramble of thoughts fled Dusty's brain, as in that moment he jerked up his eyes unconsciously. He saw something that had missed him up until now. There was a second door to the place. A door at the far end of the rear wall. And it was being pushed open, and a crouching figure holding a machine gun was wiggling inside.

No time to yell to Jack Horner! Less in which to tell the Englishman to duck down! A split second only in which to act! The figure at the door was bracing himself, raising the gun up.

Flinging out his left arm Dusty caught the Englishman across the chest and knocked him over flat on his back. In the same infinitesimal flicker of time he dived clear over the loading truck in front of him, crashed down onto the floor on his stomach, and went sliding forward like a ricocheting shell slithering along the armored steel deck of a battle cruiser.

Right hand clutching his gun, he flung himself forward and jerked the trigger twice.

The two sounds were so close that they were as one. The figure crouched in the doorway spun half way around on his knees, then fell over on his side, and the machine gun clattered down onto the floor.

Hardly had it touched the floor than Dusty was on his feet and lunging for it. His free hand grasped the barrel, jerked the gun toward him.

Something plucked at the loose sleeve of his extended arm, and a white-hot coal slid across the left side of his neck. And before his red-filmed eyes a swarm of black uniformed figures silhouetted against dull gray background, was sweeping toward him!

CHAPTER 16
THE SILVER TYPHOON

WHAT HAPPENED next was the result of impulsive, instinctive action. There wasn't even time to think. When it was over, a matter of split seconds, Dusty realized that the machine gun in his hands was spraying hot steel out through the open doorway, smashing and spinning screaming figures into the ground outside. Those who were not being mowed down were racing away in wild retreat.

A moment later, Dusty became conscious of something else happening. The Englishman had flung his arms about his chest and was pulling him back from the door, and at the same time closing it.

"Stop it, Yank—stop it! Enough—we're ready!"

Dusty staggered to his feet, looked at the Englishman. The man was waving his hand toward the row of chutes. All were loaded, and ready for the detonating timers to be set.

"Stand guard—I insist that I do this!"

The words meant nothing to Dusty, until he saw the Englishman go racing toward the far end of the chute line. Then he understood.

The Englishman, who had suffered the tortures of hell in this place, who had been one of the human experiments during its creation, was demanding the reward of destroying it with his own hands.

Death already stamped on his thin face, his body little more than bones held in place by withered skin, the man was like lightning itself as he virtually flew from loading chamber to loading chamber, reached in and turned the timing knob and streaked to the next loading chamber.

Five seconds in which to do it? The Englishman was finished and reaching for the door locking handle on the panel in practically nothing flat.

With a mighty tug he yanked it down, and the room echoed with sound as heavy doors clanged shut and geared locking lugs dropped into place. "Now, blast your rotten hearts—here's England's compliments!"

As he spoke he grasped the air-pressure release with both hands and jerked it down with every ounce of his strength.

At that moment, as though it had actually been some sort of a prearranged signal, everything became absolutely motionless, and as silent as the grave.

Hoarse shouting and the crackle of rifle fire beyond the door Jack Horner was guarding, ceased abruptly. And beyond the door beside which Dusty stood rigid, the same eerie phenomenon took place.

Every nerve, every muscle in his entire body was held rigid by the relentless hypnotic spell cast over everything.

Through half-glazed eyes he saw Jack Horner's crouching figure to his right. And to his left at the wall panel, the immovable form of the Englishman, both hands still clinging to the air-pressure release handle.

It seemed an eternity before the spell was broken by the sharp half-screaming sound of escaping air. Like the sudden ear-splitting clanging of a fire alarm jerking the fireman out of heavy slumber, so did that tell-tale hissing scream jerk Dusty out of his paralytic coma.

He was racing across the room toward Agent 10 even as his brain registered its true meaning—that one of the compressed-air chute doors had for some reason not locked in place, and that the explosion in the gun turret far beyond might backfire and flood the control station room with billowing gas clouds and licking tongues of flame—licking tongues of flame which, once they touched the explosive drums stacked near the turntable platform at the rear wall, would turn the whole place into a roaring hell of sound and utter destruction.

He was still a dozen steps from the gaping Intelligence man when sound roared in the distance, the floor rocked beneath his feet, and the entire room shook and trembled.

In that moment he lost his balance, crashed down and slid along the floor on his knees. A blast of hot air smashed against him and spun him over like a leaf in a gale of wind.

Another, almost instantaneous explosion, rocked the floor again, skidded him around and sent him crashing into his pal. Instinct and nothing else made him grab hold of young Horner and jerk him back along the floor.

The room had suddenly become filled with swirling silver smoke, and from the second compressed air chute, now minus its disc cover, a finger of flame was etching out into the silvery whirlwind.

"Run, Jack, run—must get out the other door—leads into the open—run, Jack, run!"

DUSTY WAS hardly conscious that he was shoving Jack Horner along in front of him, pounding him with frantic fists to make him move faster.

Nor was he conscious of the Englishman staggering blindly toward them in the swirling typhoon, until the man crashed into them and they all went sprawling. With berserk effort, Dusty lurched to his feet and virtually dragged the other two toward the door.

Somewhere, far out of sight, all hell was breaking loose. Crashing, thunder, roaring sound was enveloping earth and sky.

And to its echo the floor, the walls and the ceiling of the room were swaying and rocking and shaking so violently that it seemed as though the hand of God alone was holding them in place.

And then something smashed against the top of Dusty's head. Through a dazzling haze of spinning balls of colored light he saw the door. Saw it, because it was inches from him—he'd crashed into it, head-on. Somehow he found the knob, and somehow he got the door open. It was like stepping from a blast furnace into a cold storage room.

Damp, clammy mist swept against him, fogged up the eye-pieces of his gas-mask. He brushed a, hand over them, cleared them slightly and saw shadowy figures racing madly in all directions. Then something at his side cracked sound and flame. It was Jack Horner pumping hot steel at random from the machine gun he still clung to.

"Straight ahead, Yanks—charge the blighters. We've got masks!"

Even as the Englishman shouted the words he started running across the ground, firing his gun as he ran. One or two shadows in front of him crumpled up and dropped as though by magic.

But others not in range of the Englishman's gun, nor in front of Jack Horner's, were doing the same thing—dropping like flies caught in the swirling silver typhoon that raged about everything.

Dusty shouted wildly at the Englishman, went pounding after him. But the Briton was as a man gone stark, raving insane. Tattered clothes streaming out behind him, he plunged blindly forward.

With a savage burst of speed Dusty caught up with him, flung him to the ground just as a savage burst of machine-gun fire tore over their heads. Agent 10 answered it, as he dropped down beside them.

"Stick together, English!" Dusty roared at the man. "This gas is getting them. Stick together—we'll get out of it quicker that way. There's a plane waiting—"

He didn't finish the rest. The Englishman was shouting him down.

"Follow me, blast you! Follow me—motor park over there!"

Throwing off Dusty's restraining hands the man leaped to his feet again and went charging forward. Dusty cursed himself for losing his machine gun while dragging Jack Horner out of the place, and went pounding after the Englishman. It was like racing through a silver fog whipped to typhoon fury.

Figures, buildings, everything became a maze of swaying and spinning shadows.

And then, suddenly, something loomed up in front of them. It was a low shed and in front of it stood three or four Black army staff cars. But there was something else there, also. A squad of Black troops, gas masks over their faces and rifles and automatics in their hands.

For a fleeting instant Dusty saw one of them clearly—saw that the ear one the left side of his head was missing. The features were hidden behind the gas mask.

Ekar, the avenger!

REALIZATION AND action were one to Dusty. He lunged for the Englishman, who was charging straight toward the muzzles of leveled guns. But, his clawing fingers missed the man and he went sprawling on the ground. Jack Horner, at his heels, opened fire but tripped over him and came crashing down.

Winded, unable to move for the moment, Dusty could only stare glassy-eyed at the mad Englishman. And mad he was indeed. A dozen guns cracked, and his body jerked and twisted as hot steel slammed into him. But even steel could not stop him.

His own gun barking out its last few shots, he plunged right into the midst of the group, tore the guns from the hands of the nearest Black, and started pumping steel at zero range.

By that time Dusty was on his knees and scooping up the machine gun that had slid from Jack Horner's grasp.

Shouting, cursing at the top of his voice, Dusty squeezed the trigger and splashed death into the milling shapes on either side of the Englishman.

Some of them spun over and went slamming down, and the rest screamed in terror and went racing blindly off into the enveloping silver mist. And behind they left a hero of heroes slowly sinking to the ground.

Oblivious to shots cracking all around him, Dusty leaped forward and knelt down beside the quivering figure. Glazed orbs stared up at him through gas mask eyes lenses, as he cradled the Englishman's head and shoulders in his lap. The man's chest was a mass of oozing blood, the left side of his neck was raw, red flesh, and his legs were twisted grotesquely under him.

"Jack!" Dusty roared. "Give me a hand—we'll get him into the car!"

A DOZEN GUNS CRACKED AS THE ENGLISHMAN CHARGED

The Englishman tried to raise a bleeding hand, but he did not have the strength, and the hand simply quivered.

"No—no use! Take the car—Yanks! Fixed the blighters—didn't we! England—never beaten—never! Sorry—didn't get to know you better—hear your story. Too busy—weren't we—what, old thing? Yanks—give the blighters hell—cheerio!"

Dusty started to speak, but choked the words back unsaid. They would be useless now. A brave man, braver than mere words could describe, had gone to join his valiant comrades who had also given their all that England and civilization might go on flourishing. "We've done all we can! Into the car—we've got to reach Curly and Biff!" Agent 10 exclaimed.

"Right!" Dusty agreed. "Must reach Curly and Biff—that's right!"

He spun around and leaped in behind the wheel of the nearest car. Agent 10 piled in beside him, and rested the barrel of his machine gun on the top of the streamlined windshield. Seconds later, Dusty had booted the starter, meshed gears and was sending the car charging forward.

The direction he took was simply guesswork. To his left through the silver mist were dull red glows that repeatedly changed to orange and yellow and back to red again. Like countless fountains the hazy colors spurted skyward.

And each time there was a thunderous roar that made the very ground over which the car raced tremble and shake crazily. The scene of ever-changing color marked the placement of the gun turrets, and beyond them was the road that led back to the small lake where Curly and Biff were waiting.

Dusty fed the powerful engine under the hood all the hop it could take and went tearing forward through the swirling mist.

"Easy! We'll hit something!"

Suddenly, a milling mass of figures loomed up in front. Dusty swerved the car to the left, skidded around them, and I went thundering on as Jack Horner's gun snarled out a hymn of death.

A moment later a building blocked the path. In the last second allowed, Dusty swung to the left, straightened out and went streaking past, inches from the wall.

NO SOONER had the building whipped by into oblivion, than the car seemed to leap upward. For one hellish second the jar tore Dusty's hand from the wheel and the car went careening crazily off to the left. In the nick of time he got it under control and barely missed an armored car parked, or deserted, in the middle of the road.

And then, like a curtain being raised to let light through into a darkened room, the swirling silver mist ended, and they went plunging out into clear air.

Rather, it was partially clear air. For at that moment Dusty realized for the first time that the entire heavens were overcast and that icy rain was slithering down.

No wonder everything had been enveloped in silver fog. The rain had beaten smoke and gas earthward; formed a sort of blanket that hugged it close to the ground, and even refused to let it seep out to the side.

Perhaps, the swirling silver effect was the result of burning paralysis gas, or perhaps the result of its mingling with the chemicals of smoke, flame, and high explosives.

In the distance he could see that the road along which they roared swung into the road leading past the lake. Another break for the poor people!

Dusty chuckled aloud as he mumbled the thought. Then killed the chuckle in a smothered curse. Their car was not the only car eating up distance. Ahead and to the left, tearing down the lake road was another car.

It was a low-hung, semi-armored type. In the rear seat were three figures. Two more were in front.

There was something vaguely familiar about the figure beside the driver. True, he, like the others in the car, wore gas masks. But the man's figure, the shape of his shoulders and head. Could it be—

"It is!" Dusty bellowed aloud. "It's the rat—he's trying to head us off! It's Ekar—again!"

As the words poured from his throat, Dusty took one hand from the wheel, thumped Jack Horner and pointed. The Intelligence man had already seen, and guessed the same thing, and he was shifting his position so that he could bear down with his machine gun. With a quick movement, however, Dusty dragged him back into the seat.

"Down, Jack!" he shouted. "They plan to block the road, and side-swipe us with their heavier car. Keep down and aim for their tires, if you can! I think I can fool 'em!"

By now the other car had reached the intersection of the two roads, and was swinging down toward them, traveling in the exact center of the road. Sinking as low in the seat as possible, Dusty braced himself, and took a steel grip on the wheel.

In almost the next second, the other car started to slow up and edge over to their side. Holding his car in the middle of the road, Dusty let it out to the last bit of speed and burned forward as though he intended to crash straight into the other car.

Fifty yards from it! Fifteen!

"Hang on—fire at the tires!"

The instant the first word ripped off Dusty's lips, he pulled down on the wheel to his left with all his might. The engine whined and the tires screamed on the rain-soaked road as the car swerved left and shot up a shallow embankment.

Sledge-hammers pounded against every bone in Dusty's body. He thought that his wrists had been snapped in two. The streamline windshield became a maze of millions of tiny cracks.

Guns snarled sound and metallic wasps whined past his ears, and then drummed against the rear of the car as they shot over the lip of the sloping rise and came down heavily on soft ground.

While the car was still in the air, Dusty had swung the wheel hard down to the right, and when the car struck, it virtually groaned aloud in protest as it went lurching around toward the intersection of the two roads.

Seconds later Dusty sent it careening down the slope and onto the lake road. For a split second he caught a glimpse of the armored car. It was kitty-cornered across the road they had just left and teetering over on its side, its occupants sprawled out in the rain-soaked dirt.

And the reason? Dusty just barely saw it as they leaped forward out of view.

The left front tire was shredded rubber. Jack Horner's aim had been true, and the bursting tire had hurled the speeding car out of control.

Shooting a quick side glance at the Intelligence man, Dusty nodded his compliments, then switched his eyes forward again. The road was a brownish glistening ribbon that seemed to lead endlessly forward.

Along it were running groups of Black soldiers without their guns, and racing blindly away from a hell-stricken area. And as Dusty and Jack Horner went thundering by, they didn't even turn their heads. Like scared rabbits they simply jumped out of the way and kept right on without so much as losing a step in the stride. Some wore gas masks, but most of them didn't.

"Hey! To the left—you're going past!"

Jack Horner's voice filtered faintly through Dusty's ears. He jerked his head around, and saw the familiar stretch of scraggly woods that marked the lake. In his desire to get every ounce of speed out of the car he would have thundered past without knowing it.

Braking slightly he swung down on the wheel, swerved the car up off the road and onto the muddy field. Momentum alone carried the car to within a dozen yards of the woods, and then it slid to a skidding stop.

They both leaped out and went pounding through the woods. Throwing up his hands as he ran, Dusty ripped off his mask and hurled it aside. Cool, damp air flooding his lungs filled him with renewed energy and he went sprinting through the last of the trees.

And then suddenly he saw them. Saw Curly and Biff bound helplessly on the ground, and standing over them two big, cruel-faced Black soldiers. The surprise was mutual, and it was too late for Dusty to stop. He didn't even try to. He simply kicked clear of the ground and hurled his body forward.

In the next split second he had the conglomerate flash vision of blazing eyes, snarling lips and the business-end of an automatic swinging around toward him. Then there was a belch of flame in his face, a thunderous roar of sound—and he went sailing off into darkness.

WHEN HE again opened his eyes he found himself under blankets in a bed that seemed to rock gently from side to side. Standing about the foot of the bed were Curly, Biff and Jack Horner. They were all looking at him with anxious eyes. Then suddenly, Curly Brooks grinned.

"Didn't I tell you!" he shouted. "You can't hurt that guy when you hit him on the head."

Dusty blinked, raised a hand and felt about four miles of bandages wrapped about his head.

"What the hell?" he mumbled. "Where am I?"

"Aboard the U.S.S. *New York,*" grinned Curly. "And heading home, sweetheart. How do you feel?"

"Lousy!" Dusty grunted. "But what the hell happened? How'd we get here? Last thing I remember is a Black taking a pot shot at me."

"Pot shot?" echoed Jack Horner. "Hell, they both damn near

shoved their guns down your throat. Fired at the same time—missed—and then you hit them and they went flying. By that time I was close enough to take charge of things. You were a crazy fool—but thank God you were. I got tangled with a tree and couldn't have done a thing."

"But, how'd we get here?" Dusty asked.

"I'll take that bow," Curly spoke up. "After taking care of the Blacks, Jack let us loose. We piled into the ship and took off. Boy, what a mess down there on the ground!"

Dusty suddenly remembered.

"You and Biff!" he exclaimed. "You were tied up! How—?"

Curly's gesture cut him off.

"Our mistake," he grimaced. "We saw your message in the focusing plate, and came in close to shore. Both of us climbed out to give you two a lift, and *smacko*, Ekar and a couple of his lads jumped on us.

"The bum had spotted the ship from the air, and did a bit of guessing. Banged us around a bit to find out where you were. We said ixnay, and so he took a parting smack and left us with those two eggs you clipped."

"The C-Ray—"

"In perfect shape," Agent 10 said. "Got it on board now. The bum, not knowing, didn't even look at the ship."

"Nope," added Brooks. "Another one for our side. They didn't even touch the crate. And I guess that the others didn't know about it, or else what was happening on the ground was too interesting. Anyway, not one of the umpteen Black crates patrolling around gave us so much as a buzz. I climbed up through the clouds, headed west at full revs. Sighted the Second Atlantic battle squadron when we only had a couple of hours' fuel left. That was the final break for our side. We were due to miss the shore by about eight hundred miles. It would have been a long swim."

Dusty grinned, then suddenly blinked.

"Say, that reminds me!" he exclaimed. "That race we were having before all this business came up. Who collected the dough? I want my five bucks back. No dice!"

Agent 10 looked blank, but Curly arched his eyebrows at Biff Bolton, and slowly shook his head from side to side.

"Guess we'd better get the medico down here, eh, Biff?" he said. "That crack on the head is more serious than we believed. Race? Wants five bucks? The man's raving!"

Biff Bolton pulled a sad face, heaved a big sigh.

"Yeah, you're dead right!" he rumbled. "Screwy! Ain't it hell what war will do to a nice guy?"

Dusty glared at them both, then cocked an eye.

"Listen, are you two my pals?" he asked. "Would you grant me just one little promise, huh—for a pal?"

"Sure!" they chorused.

"Swell!" Dusty grinned. "Then come back in a couple of hours. I'm going to take a nap now, but in a couple of hours I'm going to collect five bucks in cash, or a hundred bucks worth of pilot hide! In two hours—pals! Now scramola!"

And with that, Dusty closed his eyes and went drifting off.

POPULAR PUBLICATIONS
HERO PULPS

LOOK FOR MORE SOON!

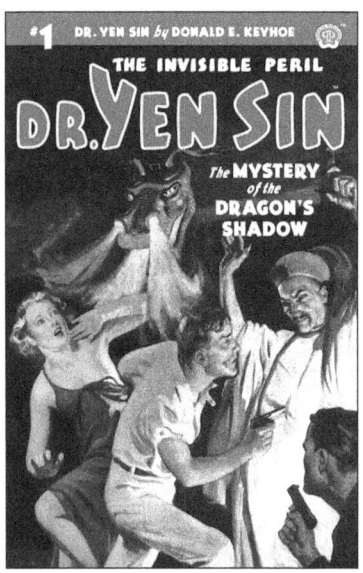

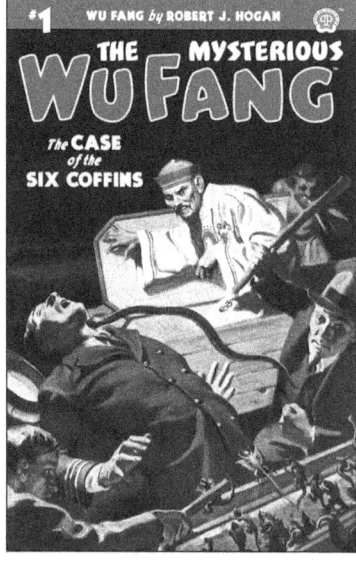